PROSE SERIES 76

MARISA LABOZZETTA

AT THE COPA

STORIES

GUERNICA
TORONTO·BUFFALO·CHICAGO·LANCASTER (U.K.)
2007

Copyright © 2007, by Marisa Labozzetta and Guernica Editions Inc.
All rights reserved. The use of any part of this publication, reproduced, transmitted in any form or by any means, electronic, mechanical, photocopying, recording or otherwise stored in a retrieval system, without the prior consent of the publisher is an infringement of the copyright law.

Antonio D'Alfonso, editor
Guernica Editions Inc.
P.O. Box 117, Station P, Toronto (ON), Canada M5S 2S6
2250 Military Road, Tonawanda, N.Y. 14150-6000 U.S.A.

Distributors:
University of Toronto Press Distribution,
5201 Dufferin Street, Toronto, (ON), Canada M3H 5T8
Gazelle Book Services, White Cross Mills, High Town, Lancaster LA1 4XS U.K.
Independent Publishers Group,
814 N. Franklin Street, Chicago, Il. 60610 U.S.A.

First edition.
Printed in Canada.

Legal Deposit — First Quarter
National Library of Canada
Library of Congress Catalog Card Number: 2006929266

Library and Archives Canada Cataloguing in Publication
Labozzetta, Marisa
At the Copa / Marisa Labozzetta.
(Prose series ; 76)
ISBN 1-55071-259-4
I. Title. II. Series.
PS3562.A2356A8 2006   813'.54   C2006-903617-9

CONTENTS

When Michael Is Away   9
At the Copa   14
Offsides   29
The Knife Lady   44
Future Games   62
The Tooth Healer   73
Surprise   88
Making the Wine   102
After Victory   112
Ticket to Ride   133

ACKNOWLEDGMENTS

Some of these stories first appeared in slightly different form in the following publications: "When Michael Is Away" in *The American Voice*; "At the Copa" and "The Knife Lady" in *VIA*; "Future Games" in *The Florida Review*; "The Tooth Healer" in *Paradise*; "Making the Wine" in *When I Am an Old Woman, I Shall Wear Purple*, and *Our Mothers, Ourselves;* "Offsides" in *Show Me a Hero*; and "After Victory" in *Don't Tell Mama: The Penguin Book of Italian American Writing*.

I am grateful to Joann Kobin, Betsy Hartmann, Mordicai Gerstein, Anthony Giardina, Roger King, John Stifler, Jeanne Schinto, Anne Halle, and the late Norman Kotker. To Scott Golub, Michele Golub, Roger Kaufman, Marty Wohl, Janet Sheppard, and Geri Pizzi, for their time and expertise. To Ariana, Carina, Michael, and Marty for their support, love, and input always. And especially to Antonio D'Alfonso – thank you.

FOR MARTY

WHEN MICHAEL IS AWAY

I walk the dog at five-thirty every day when Michael is away. Michael always walks the dog at five-thirty when he gets home from work; that and feeding the baby are the only rituals I keep when Michael is away.

When Michael is away, the house is like an old purse that has been dumped upside down and shaken free of all the gum wrappers, broken pencils and pennies. Liberated of its clutter, it is almost new. Michael is my friend, my lover, my husband.

Everything seems offbeat when Michael is away. The baby cries and cries. Just another second and she'll fall asleep, I say. I finally pick her up and she slumbers in my arms – so strong-willed and cunning is she at six months. Michael never lets her cry; he holds her until she is exhausted, and then lays her in her crib, so that she is soundly sleeping when her head meets the pillow. Michael's diapers never come undone like mine do.

When Michael is away, I use the dishwasher every day. Michael doesn't like me to use the dishwasher; he thinks it's decadent. I think so too. Michael never does the dishes.

I phone the druggist to refill a prescription. By the time I call, it is late Friday afternoon. They keep me on hold for ten minutes; I get angry and hang up. When I call back, they have gone for the weekend. Michael never procrastinates. People never keep Michael waiting.

When Michael is away, I keep the house immaculate. When Michael is home, I never seem to have much energy to clean. Michael likes a clean house. Michael is immaculate.

The baby is like me – unpredictable – or so contrary that Michael would say, "Very predictable." She grins as she yanks and tugs at my hair with a fierce grip. "Stop! That hurts!" I tell her, prying open her clenched fist. "See if you like it," I say, gently pulling a few strands of her fine blond hair. She laughs. She likes it. I have black hair; she has blond hair like Michael.

When Michael is away, my day is timeless. I awake at seven-thirty or ten. I eat a large breakfast or skip breakfast and lunch altogether. I buy prepared foods; it's exciting although I disapprove of them. I eat all the junk food I want. Not that I like junk food – I just don't like being told not to eat it. Sometimes I take my vitamins, sometimes I don't. Michael thinks it's irresponsible when I do not because I am breast-feeding. He says I am being unfair to my child. Michael doesn't need vitamins.

When Michael is away, I like to let the hair on my legs and underarms grow and grow. Michael likes it long. He says it's natural. I'll shave it before he returns because when Michael is home, I hate it long.

When Michael is away, no one asks me if I've shut the lights and locked the doors at night, but I always do. Sometimes, when Michael is home, I forget, and so he checks. I tell him he acts like my father. He tells me I act like a child.
 "I never knew you were like this," he says. "I wasn't," I tell him.

Michael and I have never been unfaithful to one another – not before, when we were living together; not now, when we are married and living together. Michael is too determined to make everything work; I am too Catholic. Sometimes, I fantasize Michael returning from one of his frequent business trips, and when we are in bed, telling me he has slept with another woman. I dramatize my reactions in my mind. I send everything on the lamp table crashing to the floor. I abruptly get out of bed and stomp into the guest room announcing that I never want to see him again. I prepare to leave him. I will never let him see the baby. I demand that he tell me exactly what transpired, then I weep with anguish upon hearing each torrid detail.

When Michael is away, I read mystery novels until the

early hours of the morning. Michael doesn't understand my passion for mystery novels. He says I do not read enough about politics. Michael reads the entire newspaper every day. I hate politics.

Michael has many projects: stained glass, painting, pottery. I like to take long walks. "You have no hobbies; that's your problem," he tells me. "I like to walk and sit in the park," I answer. You can't see a walk in the park.

About twice a year, we have a certain conversation. It varies only slightly. Michael always begins:

"What are *you* doing for this relationship?"

"What do you mean? I had a baby."

"I asked you, what *are* you doing? Not what have you done. Besides, *we* did *that* together."

"I cook and clean."

"Barely."

"I take care of the baby."

"So do I."

"Then what do *you* do for this relationship that I don't," I ask.

"I pay the bills, make all the house repairs, fix the cars, make stained glass lamps, refinish furniture . . ."

"Look, without me, there is no relationship; therefore, I *am* this relationship," I retaliate.

"So am I. You still haven't told me what you *do* for this relationship."

I am guilty, my sentence being Michael's freedom to ask the same question again in six months.

Michael says I smoke too much. He's right. He's always handing me articles on smoking and cancer, smoking and pregnancy, smoking and heart disease. When Michael is away, I never smoke. When Michael is home, I can't stop.

Michael phones once while he's away. I get excited when I first hear his voice. We talk hesitantly, almost flirtatiously – like we have scarcely spoken before. Then he asks if I have remembered to pick up the mail at the post office each morning, and I cannot wait to hang up.

I used to think that Michael was the most vital influence in my life. He introduced me to tennis, health foods and Castañeda. I never really liked any of them, but I thought I loved them. I hate them.

Michael is a good lover, but I am bored. Most women find Michael attractive; I don't notice anymore. I know I am not attractive to him. How can someone who finds you boring be attractive?

Michael is restless. I saw it in his eagerness to go on his last trip. Michael will come home and tell me he has slept with another woman, and I will say, "Oh."

AT THE COPA

"Almost ready?" Sadie Alfieri asks her daughter.

Vita slips on her Aunt Carmelina's World War II vintage muskrat coat in front of the gold-leaf bevelled hall mirror. She loves the coat. It weighs heavily on her shoulders, unlike mink or today's synthetics. Still it makes her feel luxurious, like Rita Hayworth or Ginger Rogers in *The Million Dollar Movie* shows she used to watch as a child.

"Do you have enough carfare, Vita?"

Of course, she has carfare. Why does every morning have to recall Vita's first day of kindergarten? She feels as nauseous as she did that muggy September when her mother dragged her down the center aisle of the auditorium, and she proceeded to puke in front of one hundred five-year-olds and their parents.

She begins to fasten the satin covered hooks and eyes, but stops for a moment to examine the name embroidered in beige script on the right front lining; Carmelina Passalacqua, such a long name to embroider. The coat maker must have hated her aunt. But then again, the coat maker was probably Italian and used to long names.

"You should get yourself a new coat," Vita's mother says, scrutinizing her from behind.

They never look at each other face to face, but address their reflections in the mirror and, even then, Vita tries to avoid her mother's eyes as she puts a white cashmere-like scarf around her neck. Just as good as cashmere. Feels like cashmere. But it's not cashmere. Not much in her life is authentic. Each night for the last two weeks she has dreamt of making love with a different man: the bagger at Food Town, the principal at her old school, Peter Jennings. Yet, in her conscious life, there is not the slightest sexual drive. She has become like her mother. She is a dreamer. She lifts her long hair out of the coat and lets it fall around the collar. It is *almost* the same color as the coat and gets lost among the fur. A quick glance at Vita, and one might think the coat were hooded.

"Huh, Vita? Why don't you get a new one? Always with these old clothes. I don't know what it is with you. When I was young, we were poor. We had to wear hand-me-downs. My mother would cut up my sister's old winter coats to make one to fit me, and here you are still wearing my sister's old coat. God rest her soul. Well, at least we know where it came from and what she died of. Not like those rags you get from that Praktikly Worn Shop. They could be a dead person's clothes. You would never know how they met their demise. Maybe from something contagious, or worse, they could have been murdered!"

Passalacqua, Vita thinks. Imagine if people really knew what names meant. Passalacqua – passes water or, in other words, pisses. Carmelina Pisses. She laughs.

"Go ahead. Laugh. Gives me the creeps to think of you in those clothes. And you ought to cut your hair. How long do you think you can pass for eighteen? In a few months you'll be forty. Forty-year-old women shouldn't have long hair just like fifty-year-old women shouldn't wear low neck lines. You can always tell a woman's age that way: long hair drags you down, and that crapey neck gives it all away. Hurry up or you'll be late for the Copa."

"I'm not going to the Copa, Ma. I'm going to work."

"That's what I said, the Copa."

"The Copa Cabana was a nightclub, Ma. I work at the Cabana Club. I make bathing suits." They have been through this before.

"Copa, Copa Cabana – whatever. I'll make some *aglio e olio* for dinner, okay? I got a craving. You feel like *aglio e olio?*"

"Right now? At eight in the morning? No." She catches her mother's disappointed expression in the mirror.

"Think about it at lunchtime. Work up the desire. That way when you come home from The Copa, you'll be thrilled." She starts to sing, "*At the Copa, Copa Cabana. La da da da da.* Do you remember the time your father and I went to Havana and I danced with Batista?"

How could Vita remember? She wasn't even born yet. She can barely recall her father who died when she was three. One living image. That's the only recollection she has of him. One vision of his smiling face growing larger as her baby swing with the wooden security bar that he has just pushed comes boomeranging back towards him.

"You're late," Bobby Haas says, pointing to the clock, as he unlocks the door for Vita to enter the Cabana Club, turquoise and purple walled, a fake palm tree standing in the center. The paper leaves are not so much faded as they are coated with dust making them a pale olive green.

"The bus was hijacked by Cuban midgets." Vita calmly removes her coat. Bobby smiles. He appreciates a clever lie. He is six years older than she. He's successful, attractive in a slick way (Vitalis hair, Old Spice cologne, his mandibles perpetually working away at a wad of gum), married with three children. A good catch one might have said twenty years ago; one might still say this if real mink is more important than fidelity.

Vita takes her place at one of the sewing machines in the back room of the store. She had wanted to be a social worker, but her mother discouraged her.

"It's not a nice clean job like it used to be. I remember the social worker. She was respected. When she came for home visits, the families treated her like royalty. Nowadays, those do-gooders are lucky if they leave with their lives!"

So, at thirty-nine, Vita was just as her mother had been: living with her mother, working as a seamstress. Only Vita's mother had had a child and made gowns for high fashion models in Manhattan, while Vita, never married, assembled spandex bathing suits for middle-class women in Queens.

Vita sits in a row with two other seamstresses: Svetlana, a grandmotherly rotund Russian refugee, and Antonia, a twenty-three-year-old recent arrival from Naples. They are cramped in the small quarters, and their elbows sometimes knock into one another's as they stretch and turn fabric beneath the needle shafts. A few feet away, Bobby unrolls yards of hot pink and black leopard spandex and cuts out the patterns that were custom designed to fit his clients. There is room to expand into a closet that is too big even for the hundreds of bolts of fabric stacked up high against its back wall, but Bobby refuses to give up any part of the storage area which is separated from the working room by louver doors. This is where Bobby takes inventory with Antonia, where he used to take it with Vita, where he pretends he is Sonny Corleone and his penis is the longest this side of the Hudson.

Vita can still feel the hard cardboard ends of the bolts digging into her bony back as Bobby faithfully pressed up against her, lifted a skirt or pulled down slacks, grabbed her buttocks and madly screwed her every Friday afternoon at five o'clock for years. Bobby never forced her to do it, never forces Antonia, never promised raises or jewelry or even a future, never threatened to fire her when she decided to end it. Bobby is straight that way. He has something to offer, and if you'd like to take advantage of it, everyone's needs will be met, everyone will have a good time. It put a little excitement into the work scene, provided Vita with a reason to buy sexy panties, gave her something to look forward to besides *aglio e olio* for dinner. When she found herself thinking about him before she fell asleep at night and first thing in the morning, when she began to crave the smell of his Dentyne breath, when he started kissing her before he did anything else to her, she knew it was time to stop. The phone rings at 9:55. Rosie, the salesgirl, has a bad case of stomach flu. Why didn't she call him sooner? He wants to know. She couldn't get out of the bathroom long enough, she tells him. Now, at the eleventh hour, he must make a decision. Who will be Rosie for the day? Who is most expendable from production which in his mind is always behind schedule? Each time Rosie is out, he presents himself with the same agonizing dilemma, and each time he comes up with the same logical answer. Standing in the doorway of the back room, he takes stock of the situation, while Vita has already begun to close up her machine.

Vita is his best and fastest seamstress, yet Svetlana curses the computers and the customers, and Antonia's English is still poor.

"Vita." Motioning with his index finger, he gravely summons her, as though he were about to send her down to Washington for a day in the oval office. "Rosie's out," he says.

She nods and picks up the list of appointments from the front desk.

The day is filled with *pink robes* – women who have a physical problem and must be discreetly dealt with. Instead of a white robe, they are given a pink one which, unbeknownst to them, clues in the staff on how to behave.

Ten a.m. Nancy Woodward – the mastectomy case. Vita goes into the back room and lifts the prosthesis red two-piece off the shelf. Although it's January, the schedule is booked solid and that does not account for walk-ins. It's the cruise season: Cancun, Tortola, the Grand Bahama Islands. This year everyone seems to be going to Costa Rica. A few old timers will stick to their condos in Miami or West Palm Beach. A ride across the George Washington Bridge sounds exotic to Vita.

While Nancy Woodward eagerly takes the red suit into one of the two dressing rooms, she hesitates to pull the green and white striped cabana styled curtain across the rod.

"Go ahead," Vita says, smiling. "I made it myself. Go on. My name is Vita."

She shoos her off like a child to bed. The woman takes in a deep breath and draws the curtain. While she is changing, a new client enters the shop. She is well into her fifties but convinced no one perceives her to be more than fifty-five, with her long bleached blond hair and tanning salon complexion. Vita has to admit, the hair does not drag down this svelte lady, rather it adds a sultry air to this already sensuous woman who is accompanied by a dark mustached man in his late twenties. He is more than her lover; he is her spokesperson, a Ken for this Barbie who merely smiles while he points to the sample of a string bikini pinned up on the wall. Given the opportunity to open her mouth, Barbie might confess to all: her age, his lovemaking prowess, her fat bank account.

Vita approximates Barbie's size and hands her a black dummy of the suit. After Barbie emerges from the dressing room, Vita positions her in front of a computer's camera, while Vita stands in front of the screen which projects Barbie's image. *A bun wrap*: Vita extends the fabric on the image to cover the woman's full butt with the movement and click of a mouse. *Breast firmer*: she mechanically inserts bones on either side of the skimpy cups. She clips the crotch one quarter of an inch. *Center front bottom lift*. She adds an inch to the waistline of the bikini until it skirts the belly button and covers a patch of flab.

"I think the bottom's too high," Ken says with a smirk. Vita takes off the inch she has added and an additional one that will probably leave a fringe of pubic hair showing on the finished product.

"Would you like a removable strap for swimming?"

"She'll take her chances." Ken winks.

"All set." Vita clicks off the computer. "Which do you want?" She addresses Ken who is already studying the fabrics tacked up on a wall. He chooses the silver lame. Figures. "It'll be ready in a week."

"But we're leaving for Acapulco in two days." A condo left by her late husband no doubt, probably considerably older than she, of the generation that bought in Acapulco's investment heyday. From the register, Bobby clears his throat.

"I think we can do it," Vita says. She knows the skimpy suit will take no more than half an hour to assemble. She'll stay late.

"Vita, would you take a look at this," the prosthesis client timidly calls. Vita waits until Barbie is back in the other changing room before she opens the curtain. Barbie's breasts might be a slight bit sagging, but they are big and all there.

"It's gorgeous," Vita tells her.

"You can still tell."

Vita speaks softly as the woman studies herself in the mirror. "What you are still seeing is what's inside. I can't do anything about that. But, on the outside, no one can notice a thing. You look beautiful."

The woman smiles.

"Red's a sexy color, you know. It becomes you."

Now the woman is genuinely blushing. Vita feels good.

"Save me from this one," Svetlana begins to tremble as Vita picks up an orange and white polka dot one-piece from the back shelf. "Four times I make over this suit. Four times! A magician I am not!"

They have been working on fitting Margaret Schaeflin for three months, and still the woman is not satisfied. After nearly lethal dieting, she is plump with hanging flesh all over her. Once Bobby made the mistake of telling her that they made bathing suits, not new bodies. Margaret left in a rage. A week later she was back. That was the problem; she always came back. Today she takes the suit into the changing cabana, unhappy that Rosie is not there to wait on her.

"Let me see it when you have it on," Vita tells her. After fifteen minutes, the woman calls her back in.

"It's not right. I still look fat."

Vita examines the suit; there is not much more she can suggest. They have already put on a skirt to hide her rippled veiny thighs, a drape to camouflage her distended stomach, padded cups to defy gravity and lift the breasts, giving the illusion of cleavage. She admits that a solid, perhaps black, would have been more flattering; however, Margaret has it in her mind that black is for old women, and she is only forty-eight.

"It's not right. Rosie promised me. You're all out to get me. Everyone's out to get me."

"Mrs. Schaeflin, most people are not out to take anything from you. We can refund your deposit and hope you find satisfaction elsewhere."

"Elsewhere? There is no elsewhere! There is no second chance. You people are the only game in town, and you know it. I was depending on you."

"You realize there is only so much a bathing suit can do."

"I'll have you people sued up the kazoo! Your advertisements say: *Solve Your Problems: Custom Made Bathing Suits.* My husband left me for a twenty-three-year-old. They live in my apartment building. I want to sit at the pool and make him jealous. This is my only chance." She points to the suit.

"Are you sure your body was the reason he left?"

"What do you mean?"

"I mean, maybe he was just restless. Give him a little time. I'm sure he'll wake up."

"Do you think I don't know what I see in the mirror?"

"If that's the only reason he left, then he wasn't worth it."

"Are you saying I wasted twenty-six years? Of course, he was worth it! He was my life!"

Throughout Vita's childhood her mother had exhibited nothing but disdain for men: Vita's grandfather had deserted her grandmother and eight children, leaving them to resort to stealing away in the middle of the night from one tenement to another because they couldn't afford the rent. *"Sono tutte bestie,"* her grandmother would say about the male gender – they're all beasts. Word had it that Vita's own father was less than ideal, a handsome ladies' man who spent more time puffing Di Nobili cigars and playing cards at the Caffè Paradiso than repairing shoes at his father's shop. But somewhere along the way her mother began to romanticize him and their relationship, lauding him so as a husband and provider, just stopping short of having him canonized.

"Why don't you play with it a little more and see if you can come up with something." Vita leaves Margaret alone.

"Get her out! We need the dressing room," Bobby orders.

The store is filling up with customers. Bobby splits his time running back and forth from the cash register to the pattern table at the back room.

"I can cut," Antonia says.

"Just sew!" he tells her. "Just sew!"

Margaret Schaeflin has not left the dressing room.

"I'm gonna throw her out," Bobby mumbles to Vita.

She persuades him to let her try one more time rather than cause a scene in the crowded shop, and goes into what has become Margaret Schaeflin's private cabana.

"How are you doing?"

Margaret, still analyzing herself and the bathing suit in the mirror, does not answer.

"You know, my mother used to tell me a funny story. Would you like to hear it?"

Margaret shrugs her shoulders. Vita takes the stool from the corner and sits in it.

"My mother's family comes from Bergamo. Have you ever heard of it? It's a beautiful hill town outside of Milan which can be a terribly foggy city. Sometimes the fog is so bad you have to feel around the buildings to know where you're going, and they often close down the airport. Well, my grandmother had two brothers who were very smart and very good looking: Giorgio and Stefano. My great grandfather wanted to send them to Milan to the university. They were going to become lawyers. But in those days men couldn't exist on their own; they needed to be taken care of."

"Only in *those* days?"

"Anyway, my grandfather found them an apartment, but then he had to find a woman who could cook and clean for them, do their laundry. This wasn't easy because it had to be someone who would not become involved with the boys, someone who the boys would never be attracted to. So he found this plain young girl from Bergamo, who was chaste like a nun – beyond reproach. The boys studied and paid no attention to Celestina (her name was Celestina) and she took good care of them and didn't meddle in their affairs. Then one night, Giorgio came home and heard these sounds coming from Celestina's room. He stopped in front of her closed door and listened more carefully. It was unmistakably her, grunting and moaning. When he called out to her to see if she was all right, she said, 'Oh yes, fine.' And so he went on to bed. The next morning, when my great-uncles got up, they found no breakfast made for them, no clean clothes laid out. Angry, Stefano knocked at Celestina's door. There was no answer. He opened the door and nearly fainted. There in her bed was not only Celestina, but her infant daughter who she had given birth to during the night! Of course, Celestina's mother was immediately brought to Milan. Outraged, the woman asked, 'Who did this to you?' And Celestina meekly looked up at her mother and said, 'I don't know. It was too foggy!'"

"She was a tramp."

"Exactly!"

"So?"

"Don't you see? This was supposed to be a chaste girl, a girl 'beyond reproach.' Get it?"

Margaret doesn't get it.

"The point is that things aren't always what they seem to be, or how they appear to be. What I'm saying is, maybe your husband left you for reasons you have never even suspected. When did he start to pull away from you?"

"When I began to lose weight. The more I changed, the more he changed, yet he had always complained about my being fat."

"Are you a good cook, Margaret?"

"Oh, yes I used to be – strudels, stroganoff, dumplings. But when I started to diet, I put us both on very strict menus. I don't understand why he was so miserable; he lost tons of weight too. He ended up looking so good he got a twenty-three-year-old!"

"Do you think he's happy now?"

"When I see him, he doesn't look it, but I'm sure he is."

"Why, Margaret? Why are you so sure? Do you think this new girlfriend is a good cook?"

"I doubt it. They're always going out to eat."

"You have something she doesn't, Margaret. And that's what he missed, and still misses."

"What are you saying?"

"Food, Margaret. You both loved food. That's why he left you and that's how you can get him back."

Margaret is intently listening. A smile breaks out on her face. "Have you ever made *osso bucco*?" Vita almost whispers the word and lets it magically roll off her tongue. Margaret shakes her head. "I'll give you the recipe. Try it tonight. Ask him to stop by. Better yet. Leave it at his doorstep with a sweet note that says you were thinking of him. Maybe one of those Hallmark cards." Vita runs out over to the counter where she grabs a piece of scrap paper from next to the register.

"What were you doin' in there all this time?" Bobby's jaw is so taut it barely moves as he speaks. "I thought maybe she convinced you to be her roommate."

"Shh! I'm writing down a recipe."

"You're what? Vita, the store is bustin' with customers. We have a nut hauled up in a dressing room, and you're playin' Betty Crocker!"

"No, Sadie Alfieri."

Bobby is about to grab the pencil from her when a smiling Margaret Schaeflin emerges from the cabana in her street clothes. She takes the recipe and pays Bobby the balance due on the bathing suit.

"I'm not even gonna ask, but thank you," Bobby tells

Vita. "Now go over to that redhead – another pink robe."

More mastectomies, a double colostomy (twins), skinny ladies, fat ladies, young ladies, old ladies. By the time Vita finishes the string bikini for Barbie, it's nearly six-thirty. Svetlana and Antonia left an hour ago; Bobby is rolling up several bolts of fabric.

When Vita phones her mother to say she'll be late, Sadie Alfieri informs Vita that she decided not to make *aglio e olio* afterall. She made chicken chow mein instead.

"You did good today, Vita. I'm gonna give you a raise – fifty cents more an hour. You deserve it – not just for today."

"Thanks." Those are the ones Vita usually has trouble with, the *you-deserve-it* ones, the ones for herself.

"You could use more help on the floor," she says.

"Rosie can handle it."

"It's too much for one person – even Rosie."

"You sayin' you wanna work the floor?"

"You need me there."

"I need you to sew."

She clips her last thread and turns off the sewing machine. *Just sew, Vita. Just sew.* She goes for her coat.

"You're making a mistake, Bobby."

"I'm makin' a *mistake*?"

"Yeah."

He is quiet for a moment.

"All right, all right. Two days a week you work with Rosie. I can get someone else to sew."

She smiles.

"Hey, Vita. You wanna take inventory?" He has his back to her as he puts the bolts into the storage closet. Vita knows he stays in that position in anticipation of a rejection.

"What do you say, Vita?"

"I don't think so."

He nods.

"You still get the raise, you know. And the job. You're okay, Vita." He slides the last bolt on top of the others, unable to face her.

She slips on her coat. She is hungry now.

OFFSIDES

"My father loved baseball, but he had no sons," Diana told Richard. "He did teach me how to pitch one time, but I never graduated to batting."

"I'll show you how to play soccer!" He, Richard Grossman, coach of the Chester Strikers, would give her a crash course so that on Sunday, when she came to watch her first game, his girls' game, she would not ask stupid questions of the crowd; rather, she would know exactly what was going on.

"I'm warning you," she said as they approached the vacant field. "I used to sit out family softball games in my grandmother's bathroom where I conjured up the greatest excuses not to play: from tummy aches to acute diarrhea!"

"Soccer is nothing like baseball. It's a game where everybody gets involved, where you can be creative on the field and not be limited to second base. Diana, it's a game that you play in the rain!"

"Is that why you don't use your hands – so you can hold an umbrella?"

"Funny. By the way, the league doesn't allow jewelry."

"I think my age already disqualifies me."

He would never find a female of his own generation with a passion for soccer. Perhaps that's why he looked to teenage girls. Or was it the other way around? Had all the time he spent with them taken away his need for a woman? Some years, he coached two and three teams in one season. He knew people in town thought him odd for this reason. If he were still married and had a daughter of his own, would they? Absolutely not.

He removed a ball from the large fish-net sack he carried and began to juggle it from his toes to his thigh to the side of his foot back to his thigh.

"Jog slowly with the ball, touching the center of it at every step, like this," he said.

She did as she was told. Petite, well-coordinated, from the back, she could be mistaken for one of the girls on his team. But it was clear she had no interest in what she was doing. "Girls didn't play soccer when I was growing up!" She wiped away beads of sweat from under her eyes, careful not to smudge her mascara.

He tossed the ball at her and she met it with her head, then said it gave her a headache. "How do those players keep doing it over and over? Doesn't it hurt?"

"Of course, it hurts. Sports always hurt."

"Kelly was lousy at practice today," he said as they got back into the car. "I know she's smoking pot. That senior she's seeing is trouble."

"What are you going to do about it?"

"Maybe have the girls sign an agreement not to do drugs and alcohol – but then some of them would just lie."

"You going to tell her parents?"

"There's only the mother. Anyway, I'd never betray the girls."

Diana leaned towards him. When she put her lips on his, he barely responded.

"Now, who are you worried about? This is no good, Richard. I can't compete with a dozen fourteen-year olds."

"Eighteen. A soccer team has eighteen players." He

kissed her back quickly, then started the engine. It was Friday evening, the night before the play-offs, and it was getting late. He had to go home and make his calls.

They had met at Chester Savings Bank. Triumphant after a 5-0 win, he had walked in still wearing his blue and white team warmups and safari hat that resembled the one worn by the fortune-seeking movie hero, Indiana Jones. He believed it brought him luck, and was never without it at games or practices. Besides, it hid his receding hairline. She had smiled at him as he made his way through the winding velvet ropes. Her long dark hair was pulled away from her face, emphasizing the wide grin and large straight teeth. When he stepped in front of her teller's grill, she glanced at the hat and said, "Welcome to *The Temple of Doom*."

The following Saturday, he uttered what he had rehearsed all week.

"Can I take you to lunch when the bank closes?"

"Sorry, I have a management class at the college. How about dinner tonight?"

Her forwardness pleased him, yet made him anxious. Plus, she was ambitious. What would she say when he told her he'd been sorting Zip codes in the Chester Post Office for the last nine years? His ex-wife used to slip continuing education brochures in between the pages of his *Soccer America*.

Settled in his condo, a converted textile mill, Richard began to dial. Jenny K., Jenny O., Cara S., Cara M. – he flipped through his mental Rolodex. Did anyone name their daughters anything other than Jenny, Cara, or Sara anymore? Whenever a coach yelled out one of those names at a game, at least five heads turned.

First he called Ana, his steady one, a solid defender and a great assister. The perfect teammate, she knew how to make the girls talk to each other on the field.

"I saw you downtown with your new girlfriend tonight," she told him. "You were skipping in front of City Hall."

"I skipped twice." It was one of what he liked to call his "rambunctious" moments – those urges he insisted acting upon, believing they'd keep him young.

"You were skipping all the same. Pretty lame, Grossman."

He'd been trying to keep his affair with Diana a secret. People were accustomed to seeing him alone. Grossman, the *girls'* soccer coach, tall and thin, with his khaki pants and red suspenders, sandy hair slicked back like his NBA coaching idol Pat Riley's. Lately, the sight of him with Diana was drawing extended stares from people who knew them. His compulsion to hide every time they encountered one of his girls aggravated his awkwardness in public. He just didn't know how to work Diana into his image. Perhaps that was what had gone wrong with his marriage; maybe he had never known how to fit a real woman into his life.

"And what did you think?" he asked.

"You were good, Grossman. You shot across the street before I could see your girlfriend's face."

"Go to sleep early. No babysitting this weekend. No sleepovers. No dates. Seven-thirty we meet in the bowling alley parking lot. Your parents coming?"

"Yup."

"Excellent. Most of you will need rides."

The girls had arrived at the Ludlow game half asleep last Saturday, stepping out of station wagons and vans with their warm-up jackets hanging off their shoulders. After stretching out, they looked as if they wanted to lie back down and curl up on the green. The Ludlow girls were already fiercely engaged in passing and shooting drills.

"Don't stand around!" he'd shouted. "Run! Get a ball! Get out there and juggle, but don't stand around!" It had irritated him to see them like that, because it was exactly what the old boys at the Recreation Department were always screaming about: girls didn't take athletics seriously; girls were not worth the time, the effort and, especially, not the money.

Kelly had looked the worst of all of them that morning, her big green eyes reduced to slits. Sluggish throughout the game, she had obviously been up late with her boyfriend. The Strikers lost, but it hadn't only been Kelly's fault.

"Second half teams are losing teams," he had told them afterwards. "Ludlow played a very clean, aggressive game. You've got to go in harder, girls. The harder you go in, the safer you are. You had your share of opportunities. You were outplayed. But we've got another chance at them in the play-offs. A little more commitment to be in there first, and we'll take it. Anybody got any thoughts, comments?"

"Yeah." Ana punched a soccer ball lying next to her. "How do we *really* beat Ludlow next week?"

"You beat them by taking shots. More shots at the top of the box. Next week I want everybody up. Push 'em out of there harder and faster. Wings can't trail behind the sweepers and fold."

Exhausted, Kelly had asked him for a piggy-back ride to the parking lot, and he had given it to her, despite a disapproving look cast by Ana's mother. This "rambunctious" moment might have been wrong, but Richard liked to take care of Kelly, maybe because she had no father. She was naive, different from some of the other girls. Leslie, whose wild curly red mane was never secured in a ponytail, enjoyed lying on the ground propped up on her elbows during pep talks, knowing full well Richard could see down her V neck jersey. Once she had fallen and pulled up her shorts to show him the strawberry on her rear end.

Belligerent, hostile, Liza was his real problem, though. When she was on, she was a great player; when she was off, a total disruption to the team, leaving a big gaping hole in the middle of the field, because if the center half isn't doing her job, the entire team falls apart. Once, when she was accidentally tripped by her own teammate, she went into such a rage they had to carry her off the field. That won her a yellow warning card from the referee. Another time, a teammate and she tried to win the ball; Liza whacked at the girl's ankles, threw elbows, just lost it.

One by one he phoned them all. He had no idea what their parents thought about the calls, although he once overheard Liza's mother say, as she handed the receiver to her daughter, "Tell him to get a life." What was the problem? Coaching was a serious endeavor. They wanted good teams? Winning seasons? Well, this was part of it.

Coaching fourteen- and fifteen-year-olds meant getting into their heads, reading their minds on and off the field, teaching them to trust him enough so that when he sent them out to perform, they had faith in his judgments, in themselves. Something happened to girls at their age. Just when they were beginning to believe they could do it, they turned self-conscious on him. Then, one by one, they dropped out, feeling more comfortable on the sidelines of some boys' competition.

Now, it was the boys who had started cheering Grossman's teams, and lately that wasn't sitting so well with the recreational powers that be – the old boys' network of middle-aged men whose families had run the town's sports for generations. Richard wasn't sure whether they hated him more for having instituted the Chester Soccer Club, which drew players away from "real" sports like baseball and football, or for not having the guts to coach boys. He had introduced fall soccer into the Recreation Department, but they opposed his organizing spring teams. Fall was as far as they'd allow him to go. If kids didn't want to play baseball, then they should ride a bike, was their opinion. But Richard, who had gotten into soccer because he hadn't made his high-school baseball team, and because he was too short for basketball and too slight for football, had organized his own club in Chester, one that hooked into a larger area league. On a Saturday morning in October, seven years ago, he turned up at the Rec Department soccer jamboree in his VW Rabbit, opened the sun roof, and held out a sign that said: *Spring Soccer Sign Ups.* Ninety-three boys and girls lined up to give him their names. The director of the Rec Department approached Richard's car and slapped his hand down on the hood. "Just what are you doing, Grossman?"

"Excuse me, but I'm a taxpayer. Please move aside because there are a lot of people trying to sign up."

Since then, each fall and spring he laid out the field: ten yards here, seventy there; ran the corners square; measured off the boxes around the goals; marked it all with string and pegs. Then he hauled two tons of lime in eighty-pound bags onto the green, filled the lining machine, and walked the perimeter. If the ball went beyond those lines, it was out of bounds – clear and simple. Some plays were trickier to call, however. One minute you could be onsides, ready to receive a pass, when the defender pulled up on you. Before you knew what had happened, the referee was calling "offsides," and awarding the other team a big fat indirect kick.

He hadn't always coached girls but, when spring soccer first began, the fifteen-and-under girls' team was stranded. If he hadn't taken them on, they wouldn't have played. Each season thereafter, the girls begged him to continue.

He wouldn't go back to boys now; they were too cocky. The girls let him care about them; he let himself care about them.

After he had made his last call, the ringing of the phone startled him.

"Good luck tomorrow," Diana whispered. "How about dinner tomorrow night?"

"I'll call you after the game – Diana?" He wanted to tell her that he loved her; he had wanted to the last few times they'd been together, but he couldn't. He used to tell his ex-wife he loved her all the time, and what good had it done? She had gotten up one morning, told him they had nothing in common, and left. He thought he had learned something from his failed marriage: keep the dearest sentiments within. But this was difficult to do with Diana. She was the first person since his high school soccer coach who made him feel he was good enough.

Tonight his passion was there, ready to be expressed through the telephone wires. "Like I just finished telling all my girls, get a good night's sleep," he said instead.

It poured on the first day of the play-offs, a cold hurricane-like Saturday in the middle of June. By the time the girls stepped onto the field, their cleats sank deep into the mud. They were hungry for a win however. Enjoy the game, sure, but victory is what it's really about.

Within the first five minutes, Ludlow scored. His girls were faster, Richard had no doubts; they beat Ludlow to the ball each time, but Ludlow was bigger, and now with a wounded ego, Richard feared the Strikers would give up the ball too easily. Towards the end of the first half, Sara B.'s father, who liked to coach from the sidelines, pacing to and fro, hands on his fat hips, confusing the hell out of the girls, shouted to his daughter as she lost the ball, "Sara, if you can't get tough, go home!" No sooner had Mr. B. made his proclamation than Sara sent the ball in. And it would have been over by the end of the the second half – the Chester Strikers would have taken it neatly – had it not been for the weather conditions. Balls react differently to water than they do to dry ground. Cara S. dribbled the ball down the wing and crossed it high to Jenny K., who headed it to Kelly. With the goalie out of the box, Kelly booted it in; however, instead of rolling, the ball stopped short as it smacked into the puddle that had formed around the entire goal. And there it sat, waiting for the Ludlow goalie to lunge at it before Kelly could come in for a second kick.

Double overtime went into penalty kicks; Jenny K.'s mother walked back to her car, unable to watch. After Ludlow had taken five shots and Chester four, they were tied at three goals. Then Liza stepped up, kicked into the upper left-hand corner of the net, and the first game of the play-offs was over. Afterwards, Richard had wanted to scoop Liza up and kiss her, but some calls were harder to make than others. Whenever he had complimented her on her performance before, she had become overconfident and screwed up in the next game.

"Nice job!" he congratulated her. She stared at him, full of expectancy; he just smiled, and chose to say nothing more.

They were sitting in Hunan Palace when Richard nonchalantly suggested to Diana that she not come to the Springfield game the next day.

"Why not?"

"You've never come to a game before. Why start now?"

"Because the season's almost over."

"It *is* over. These are play-offs," he reminded her.

"Whatever. It's a game, right? The last game."

"I still can't spend the night with you."

"Richard, I already know all that. No sex before games."

"Correct, an early night."

"How about early sex?" She grinned.

"Can't."

"Will you pick me up in the morning?"

He shook his head. He was getting that familiar feeling he always got with women – the fizzle that followed the sizzle and which usually came no later than after the second date. That his relationship with Diana had lasted so long astounded him, for, at the moment, she might as well have been some stranger sitting across from him. What had he seen in her anyway? Too much lipstick, too much jewelry. To think, he had almost told her he loved her.

"Fine. I'll come on my own. Give me directions." He scribbled them out on a napkin. "Are these directions to the field or a way out of a labyrinth? You don't want me to come, do you?"

"It's not *you*, it's just – I'm on a winning streak. I can't break it. You've never come to a game this season and we're seven and one."

"Now I'm bad luck? Is that what you're saying?"

"Sort of. But it's not only luck. It's the girls. They haven't seen you before. If you show up now, it might throw their concentration."

"It's not that you don't want them to see me, is it? It's that you don't want *me* to see *them*!"

Richard doesn't answer.

"All your talk about my getting interested in soccer is a bag of bullshit, isn't it, Richard? You like that you have your idolizing girls all to yourself. You don't want them to see that there's anybody else in your life and you certainly don't want me to meet them because they *are* your life! You want them to think you're theirs alone! They're almost women, Coach, and whether you like it or not, they're going to leave you. Soon, Richard. They always do."

She was crazy – way off base, he wanted to believe, but

he knew better. He had to stop her from saying another word.

"Let's get out of this place," he said.

Later, he felt bad as he pulled in front of his apartment. Why did Diana frighten him? "The harder you go in, the safer you are. You win by taking shots," he always told his girls. *You win by taking shots. You are a coward, Richard Grossman. You are a loser.*

The Chester Strikers managed to hold the Springfield Comets back the entire first half. Goaltender Leslie took a dive for the ball at the same time the Springfield forward followed through with a kick that met Leslie's trachea. She scared Richard the way she lay absolutely still on the ground. When the ref called him over, he didn't know what to expect; as he neared her, she lifted her head. Her jersey had become twisted around her torso, and one of her breasts was partially exposed through the shirt's neck-opening.

"Want a sub?" Richard asked.

"Nope."

He was relieved. None of the others could punt like Leslie; she was agile and fearless – had great hands. At halftime it was zero-zero.

"Always, always try to be first," he told them as they squirted water into their mouths. "If you can't, play the pressure and get that ball under control. If you can do that and have every player on the field marked, then we'll do fine."

They kept the field compact; they pressured. Their traps were the finest he'd seen all season. Then it happened. Sara B. and Liza went after the ball, but Sara B. won it and scored. Richard could see by the scowl on

Liza's face that he had made a lousy call the day before; he should have commended her more on her winning penalty kick.

At the restart, Liza and a Springfield player engaged one another in a series of name calling; the referee told them both to cool it. Volatile Liza wouldn't. "Put a lid on it, Liza!" Ana warned from midfield. That's when Liza held up her middle finger to Ana; the ref, in turn, gave Liza a red card and threw her out of the game.

Even with his team down one player, Springfield failed to score – until the last minute.

"Everybody up! Hustle!" Richard called as Springfield took off on a breakaway. They remained solid. Had they missed opportunities? Sure. Still, they had nothing to be ashamed of, and they felt good about that.

With the whistle blown and the hands slapped, the anxiety of a season was unleashed for all – players, parents, coach.

No one had noticed Diana standing on the other side of the field with the spectators. She wore tight jeans, a white tank top, and gold hoop earrings. Her face was made up and her hair perfectly styled. Now, she stood out among the girls dripping with perspiration and the worn-out looking mothers in their baggy shorts and T-shirts. As Richard crossed the field, she approached him.

"I'm sorry," she clumsily offered.

"Yeah, tough one." He looked down at the ground, then back up at her, still surprised to see her there after the awkward way they had parted the night before. They were smiling at one another, not saying a word, when Leslie crept up behind Richard and threw a large thermosful of cold water at his back.

"Got you, lover boy," she giggled.

He tore off after her, almost circling the entire field, his good luck safari hat long fallen from his head. They were just about back in the center of the crowd when Richard caught her from behind by grabbing at a fold in her jersey and pulling her, face down, onto the ground. In a "rambunctious" moment, he straddled her, then picked up the cooler next to them, and poured melted ice water over her mass of red hair while she laughed and wiggled beneath him, her buttocks bobbing up and down, her breasts bouncing against the earth.

It wasn't the water that shocked the onlookers. They had grown silent just as he climbed over her. When he became aware of the stillness, he lifted himself off, and met the confused gazes of parents. He had grossly misjudged his position; he had been offsides and out of bounds all at once. Word would reach the board members of the Rec Department, and they, in turn, would seize the opportunity to have him canned from the Soccer League. Even if his thoughts were running away from him, one thing he knew was certain. The story would spread around gossipy Chester; word of mouth would keep the incident alive and make future soccer players' parents wonder if they should let their daughters be on Grossman's team.

Once again, he had lost sight of Diana, until suddenly she was standing beside him. She held out a hand; with the other, she dragged his sack of soccer balls. She wore his warm-up jacket draped over her shoulders, the arms tied around her neck, and his too large hat floated on top of her head. Seeing her, he found the courage to speak. He thanked them all, parents and players alike, for a great season, and he told them he'd meet them again next fall.

"There'll be tryouts," he warned with a coach's decorum. Then he took the sack from Diana and hoisted it over his shoulder. "You smell good," he mumbled, wrapping his free arm around her and leading her away from the crowd, his eyes fixed on the parking lot.

THE KNIFE LADY

"If you want to cook properly, you must have the correct utensils. Sharp knives, Joan. They're essential," Stephanie whispered to me at one of her dinner parties.

Stephanie ought to have known. She certainly had all the right gadgets. Her sanitized white kitchen looked like a page out of *Chef's Magazine* with an assortment of shiny copper pots dangling from a heavy brass rack directly above a Jen-Air range. I often wondered what she used to attach it to the ceiling. I had trouble keeping pictures on the wall.

"Gas," she said. "Gas is best to cook with but electric is where it's at for baking – heats more evenly. You don't get those burnt edges." Stephanie had three ovens: gas for roasting, electric for baking, and convection for whatever they're for. I never had those "burnt edges" she was always talking about. I never baked.

"Not even a mix?" Stephanie said at the school bake sale, recognizing that my cupcakes had been purchased from the supermarket.

"Who needs a mix when there's Entenmans, Freihoffers, Sara Lee?" If company was coming for dinner, I prepared the meal hours ahead of time, cooking it and serving it in the same Corning Ware pots. That way, I was never confused when guests arrived, never forgot the salt or the eggs, never had serving dishes to clean up. Casseroles were my favorite. As long as you had all the right ingredients, it was bound to turn out edible, no matter how it went into the baking pan, and, when you dished it out onto the plates, a lump was a lump and needed no fancy arranging. Stephanie, however, didn't even start to cook until her guests arrived. Just as the last person entered, she began hauling out odd pieces of meat, vegetables, herbs, things I'd never even seen before in their raw state. Suddenly, she was madly slicing and chopping away, right in front of you, on her authentic four-legged butcher's block, talking to you all the while about the latest city council scandal. Her meals elicited comments from my monolingual husband like. *Delizioso! Magnifique! Wunderbar!* The only adjective Manny ever applied to my cooking was an occasional *good*. So when the knife lady said she was a friend of Stephanie's, I gave her telephone time at six p.m., and later welcomed her into my home.

We were in the middle of digging into a bowl of my chili – my son complaining it had been on the menu for three consecutive weeks; my daughter declaring that the kind in the can was better – when the phone rang.

"Sure," I said. "I'd like to see your knives." My family looked up at me with sudden trepidation, *sorry* written all over their faces.

"What kind of knives?" Manny asked after I'd hung up.

"How many kinds of knives are there?"

"Well, there are carpet knives, and – "

"Machetes!" my son threw in.

"These are plain knives, Manny. *Kitchen* knives."

The image of the Fuller Brush Man at my mother's Brooklyn apartment door quickly evaporated when Kate appeared the following afternoon that summer. She was tall and lean in a pair of white shorts, like a gazelle, and, although I'd never even seen the animal, I knew the comparison was accurate. Her skin was slightly tanned to give just the right contrast to her short platinum pageboy. The blue tank top emphasized her eyes which were blue like the little flowers on my cookware. She held a large thick leather briefcase in one hand while she extended the other with its long slender fingers and unpolished nails. I felt whorish next to her, like a short painted lady with my red lipstick, black hair, my olive skin and cellulitic thighs, my broad hips and corpulent rear end. Not that I'm fat. I'm more like a curvacious peach that's been lying around the fruit bin too long. But she, with her boyish slender hips and tiny unbridled mounds beneath her tank top, was all-American ageless. I let her in.

Seated in my living room, her legs seemed restricted between the sofa and the coffee table. She was Goliath visiting the land of trolls, and I felt that, at any moment, her lengthy arms and torso might spill over me and the entire couch. She said she was hot and tired yet she looked so cool. This woman never sweat. I offered her a drink. I knew she wanted iced tea. In Brooklyn, people still request a cup of coffee on days like these, but I've learned that here in New England, you offer Yankees iced tea.

The idea was to get the promotion over with as soon as possible: listen to Kate's spiel, tell Stephanie I tried my best to improve my culinary skills, but not buy anything.

"I'm a Jennie Carlson scholar," she began. That meant

she was matriculating at the local college thanks to a generously endowed program for mature women. "This is how I support myself, and summer is my biggest chance. After that I'm too busy with school."

She was business-like in her approach which conflicted with her tennis-court appearance. As she removed a black felt board from her suitcase and placed the display on the coffee table, I learned that these were no ordinary knives, but the best. *The best.* I hate that expression. Manny uses it all the time: this ice cream's *the best;* that Mexican restaurant's *the best.* Best is subjective. Best is contrary to fact. But somehow when Kate used it, I believed her. How could you not think that handles bound with the same stuff as airplanes are and shaped to your hand's grip weren't the best? That I didn't know what any other kind of knife was made of seemed irrelevant. Her tone was matter of fact, no hype: *You see it, you get it, or you're an idiot.*

The advantage of each piece of cutlery was multitudinous. A single spatula with a serrated edge could be used to mince celery and hard boiled eggs, scoop mayonnaise, stir the mixture, spread it onto bread, and then cut the sandwich in half. She took out small pieces of three-quarter inch leather and piled them on top of one another. She told me to get a steak knife of mine and try to cut through. My cheap knife merely made an indented line on the top layer; the *CutAbove* knife, however, sliced right through all that cowhide. "And of course, you don't serve leather," she reminded me. Little did she know. The climax followed. She handed me a penny and a *CutAbove* scissor and asked me to cut the penny in half. I did.

What I had been told would be a twenty minute presentation lasted an hour. I purchased the most expensive and complete set of knives *CutAbove* had to offer, only after Kate had thrown in a cutting board and sharpener.

"You're a good saleswoman, Kate," I said.

"You're a wise consumer, Joan." She smiled, and I felt rewarded for the five-hundred-dollar business I had just given her.

As she packed up weary from her demonstration, I tried to think of other things to offer her that might entice her to stay a little longer: a piece of my son's left over birthday cake, some Jello. Maybe we could get to know each other better, become friends. She politely declined; she was watching her weight for her next triathlon.

"Do you work out?" she asked. Her eyes were magnificent.

"I play a little tennis," I lied.

"That's something I'd like to do more, but I just don't have the time. Your knives should arrive UPS in about two weeks." She zippered her briefcase.

She wasn't delivering them; I was disappointed. She stood in the doorway and was shaking my hand just as Manny pulled up. How foolish he looked coming home from work in a pair of jeans and a baseball cap, wiry grey hair sticking out beneath the blue hat on either side of his head. His paunch gave away that he was not one of the local minor league players. One glance told Kate all: the man had no taste. I didn't bother to introduce them. He nodded and walked past us with an air of more important things to attend to like mowing the lawn. I wondered if Kate had any children. She wasn't married; she had said this job was her sole source of income.

"Thanks again, Joan. And be careful not to cut yourself! They're really sharp!"

She smiled for the first time, and I thought that maybe she did indeed like me after all, and not only because I had bought her wares.

I was preparing dinner, holding a plump ripe tomato in my hand, trying to decide whether to slice it or cube it, when Manny seemed to come out of nowhere, reach around me with his long arm, dip into the bowl of salad, and snatch several pieces of carrot.

"How do you like your tomatoes?" I asked him.

"Ooh, baby, just like you." He squeezed my rear end.

"I mean *this* tomato."

"Makes no difference to me."

"You must have a preference. Do you like it in wedges or tiny squares or rough chunks?"

"Jo, I don't give a damn."

"You don't give a damn about much."

"What the hell are you talking about?"

I didn't know what I was talking about. All I knew was that he irritated me by putting his hands into *my* salad, taking what he wanted without asking, then acting as though he had just pulled off *The Great Train Robbery*. I kept thinking of how he had come into the house not much earlier and so assuredly walked by Kate, his smugness reminding her that this was his house, and anyone beside me and the kids was just there on a pass. He too was Brooklyn through and through. I could dress him up, but I could never extract eighteen years of Boro Park living. Most of the time I couldn't even dress him up. Even worse was the fact that at moments like these, he knew exactly how much his behavior exasperated me, and so he played it up all the more.

"Who was the broad at the door?" he asked.

"The knife lady."

"Buy anything?"

"Yup. Want to know how much?"

"Nope. Let me be surprised when the Visa statement comes."

Manny is good that way. He puts no restrictions on me financially. Of course, why should he? I teach twenty-eight first graders ten months of the year and get paid for it. Still, I know lots of men who, despite their wives' income, feel a need to regulate every expenditure. Not Manny though. Nothing bothers Manny. Not until a day when the racks at his dry cleaning shop appear sparse, or too many cars are sitting in his car rental lot. That's when he'll remind me about the five hundred dollar set of knives.

"Wasn't she beautiful?" I said.

"Who? The knife lady?"

"Yeah."

"A block of ice. I caught a chill as I walked by her." He faked a shiver.

"You only saw her for a minute during which you weren't exactly warm yourself, you know."

"I was afraid to be. She might have melted like the Wicked Witch of the West." He laughed at his own joke, that annoying laugh of his that goes on and on, interrupted at intervals by an asthmatic wheezing sound.

I decisively sliced the tomato in half. From one, perfectly shaped fleshy ovary, I had created two. I matched them back together.

"Need some glue?" He was behind me once more, this time his arms encircling my waist, his lips nibbling at my neck. I ignored him and concentrated on my tomato. Glue indeed. Making it whole again was of no interest to me. There were two now, two distinct pieces, equal in every way, that fit perfectly together.

That night I stared at Manny after he had fallen asleep and I wondered who this man lying beside me was. I believed that when I had walked down the aisle all those years ago, I must have been suffering from a form of dementia. It was the familiarity that had drawn me to him in college. Two New Yorkers in a quaintly static New England college town. Two fish out of water who would leave our beds at one in the morning and drive fifty miles for good Chinese food. Two people whose thoughts superseded our speech that was pronounced with an accent only we ourselves understood. I had been attracted to sameness, but we were never really the same; we had only come from the same place. Perhaps, behind my gregarious facade lay dormant a block of ice who desperately longed to sip cool tea in the chaise lounge of a rose garden rather than hot coffee on a stool at Chock full o' Nuts. Despite my complaining about the unfriendly Yankees, wasn't it I who had secured the first job here, found the right colonial, learned to eat supermarket frozen bagels? If I had had the nerve I would have quit teaching a long time ago and opened a flower shop with roses as my specialty. Red, yellow, tea, even white roses. The florist downtown was for sale and lately I had been fantasizing about buying it, even had a name picked out – *Jo's Bloomers*. I'm not a natural with plants, but I could learn. Manny told me we didn't need two business people in the family. He said it wasn't high powered women men needed; they just wanted to be loved. Besides,

I'd been teaching first grade for so long, I had it down to a science. The September before I hadn't even gone in a day early to fix up my room. I just waited until the first day of school and let my students do it. Called it: *Hands on.* The principal loved it!

Kate probably had a great rose garden and, if she lived in an apartment, she undoubtedly had window boxes flourishing with geraniums and herbs. I thought about the length of her torso; I dressed her in a tiny black spandex bikini. I undressed her until I imagined her with nothing at all except white skin in the shape of a bathing suit. I began touching the boyish body that lay positively still and willing. What would Manny have thought if he could read my mind? He had been the reluctant one, afraid to get married because he thought he might not be able to spend the rest of his life with one woman. Now, it was that very woman who was thinking about another woman. But I was just thinking. That is the great thing about a mind: it need never open the door to anyone, never leave home. I was sitting on Kate's lap, about to rub my breasts against her adolescent-like ones, when Manny nuzzled up to me. Growing more passionate, he climbed on top of me and began kissing me. I lay there observing this wild phenomena when suddenly his eyes opened slightly and, as though coming to his senses on the verge of committing murder, he flung himself off of me and over to his side of the bed only to fall back into deep sleep.

At first, I found this behavior amusing, almost endearing. It was as though he had, in his unconscious state, become the recipient of my sexual vibes and had tried to accommodate me. However, I realized that it might be his own dreams which had aroused him, and that recognition of me, the wife, had only resulted in distress. The truth needed no further explanation. Manny was dreaming about another woman. He was having an affair.

"Wake up!" I poked at his love handles.

Startled, he sprang to a sitting position and looked at the alarm clock on his nightstand. "Jo, are you crazy? It's two-thirty!"

"I don't care. I want to talk."

"Not now. I have to get up in three hours." He slid back down under the sheets.

"Now! I want to talk right now! Who were you dreaming about?"

"I wasn't dreaming."

"Who were you thinking about?"

"No one! I was sleeping!"

"Manny, am I feminine and demure enough for you?"

"Demure ladies wouldn't jab me in the ribs and wake me at two-thirty in the morning." He grumbled, drifting back to sleep.

I tried to picture Kate doing to Manny what I had just done. I couldn't.

The next morning, I phoned Stephanie, and asked her to play tennis.

"We don't play tennis," she said.

"Let's start."

"I have Jessica today."

"Bring her along. I have Alex."

With the children in the back seat, a bag of snacks to entertain them, we drove over to the tennis courts at the high school. Jessica was coy, barely acknowledged Alex. Never does.

"Want one?" Alex held out a cherry juice box. In the rear view mirror, I could see Jessica shake her head. "You like pretzels?" He was trying so desperately. Again the head.

"Say, no, thank you," Stephanie instructed her daughter.

"No, thanks," she said with effort.

Suddenly Jessica was me and I her, a stuck up five year old who refused to kiss Nikki Laperruta, the little girl who lived in the apartment across the hall. We played together for what seemed like an eternity in the tiny bedrooms of hers or mine. We used to do things to each other, like stick the tops of perfume bottles up one another's *toushies*, then sniff them and laugh.

One day, when Nikki and I were hugging, she went to kiss me on the lips; I pulled away. Nikki started to cry. And what did I do? I ran across the hall back to my own apartment. Soon after that we both went to kindergarten; it was never the same. I've always been sure it wasn't school that caused the separation as much as my rejection of Nikki which I have never forgotten nor stopped regretting. She had just wanted me to kiss her. Such a little thing.

My good friend at school is the sixth grade teacher George. His lover's name is Art. I once asked George when he knew. He said he'd always known, but he became certain in fourth grade, when he fell in love with his classmate Mike Fitzpatrick.

"I bought the knives from your friend," I informed Stephanie.

"From *who*?"

"Your friend – Kate."

"The knife lady? She's not my friend. Actually, when

she called me, she said she was Ellen Morrison's friend. I guess that's how she gets her foot in the door."

"You don't know anything about her?"

"Not a thing. I just bought a cleaver from her. I already have so many knives."

Stephanie, the gourmet, had bought one cleaver, and I, the *shlemiel*, had spent five hundred dollars! I thought about Manny and the Visa bill, then I thought about Manny and his lover. I felt nauseated.

"Do you really want to play today?" I asked Stephanie.

"I thought *you* did."

Stephanie was an attractive woman but, to my relief, I had no desire to sleep with her. Then again, I hadn't wanted to make love with every man I'd ever known either. I asked Stephanie if she wouldn't mind keeping Alex for the afternoon. She agreed without question; Yankees don't pry.

First, I drove downtown to the dry cleaners. They told me Manny had left for the car rental. The car rental business is in another town about a twenty-five minute ride on the interstate. How fortunate for him. If Manny were having an affair, it wouldn't be with someone local. When I got to the car rental, the manager told me Manny had gone out and probably wouldn't be back for the rest of the day. I drove to some of the spots where he had lunch and searched for his car: the Easy Diner, Bickfords, Friendly's. Then it dawned on me that he would never take anyone except me out to lunch at places like those, so I hit all the nicer restaurants I could find. In desperation I found myself driving in and out of every motel parking lot on the commercial strip. When I stopped for gas at Dairy Mart, I bought a cup of coffee and drank it in the car. There, the saddest thought came to me. If Manny was with another woman at that moment, as long as the specifics were unknown to me, I didn't really care. I pushed the affair business out of my mind. Stephanie would never speculate about something so nebulous.

My knives arrived late one afternoon, just as I was about to mold a mountain of chopped sirloin into patties. Suddenly I was inspired to prepare something more creative, something that required using at least one of my new toys. I removed each knife from its bubbled plastic wrapping, washed it, wiped its mirror-like blade with a dish towel, and slipped it into the designated slot on the knife block as indicated by a diagram in my owner's manual. I could wait no longer. With my left hand I picked up one of the hard rolls Manny preferred to hamburger buns. With my right hand I pulled the long sleek bread knife from the block like a sword from its holder and proceeded to slice, through the roll, right on through the skin between my thumb and forefinger, barely missing a nerve. It happened so fast, quicker than the time it took for my regular knife to penetrate thin crust. I am a poor clotter, and used up the remainder of a roll of paper towels before I drove myself to the emergency room where I received five stitches.

"Don't anyone touch these knives! Ever!" I warned later that evening during the supper Manny had finished on the barbecue.

"Not even me?" Manny asked.

"No!"

"Why not?"

I knew Manny couldn't care less if he ever used one of these knives, as he was even less prone to cooking than I was. I had wounded his pride, equated him with having no more competency than the children.

"They're lethal weapons, Babe." I said. But that wasn't it. I didn't care if Manny cut himself. The knives were mine alone. They were special, like Kate, and I didn't want anyone else to share them. Now, the bandage on my hand and the scar that might remain would be a constant reminder of her.

Manny is not a particularly big man, but his bones – knees, ankles, elbows – are strong and dense like those of a Doberman pinscher we once had. Even when he is trying to be his most tender, they uncomfortably bang into me, keeping me on constant guard. Lovemaking with Manny came easily that night however, my imagination fast at work. When I reached orgasm, my secret unfolded with a single utterance.

"What did you say?" He lifted himself. His elbows locked, he held his body above me and asked again.

"Just a moan. You like me to make noise."

"But you said a name. A woman's name."

"Maybe it was Stephanie."

"Too long."

"Maybe I said Manny."

"It was one syllable.

"For God's sake, maybe I said *Man*."

"You never call me *Man*."

"You're being ridiculous." I took the offensive. He rolled over onto his back.

"It sounded like Fay, or Kay. Something like that," he addressed the ceiling. "How could you, at such a time be thinking of anything else let alone a woman?"

I have always thought men tended to be presumptuous and egotistical, but this last statement of Manny's provoked me to laughter. Had he really thought that each and ever time we had made love over the years, my brain was consumed with thoughts of him?

"You always tell me to let my mind go," I said.

"Not to a woman!" I could feel the tension in his body, though we were not even touching. I tried to stop laughing.

"Manny. I don't understand. When two women are making love in a porno movie, it's a turn-on to men. Why not to women?"

"They're actresses. They just do it for the movie. Besides, they're not my wife!"

"I want to know, Manny. Why is watching two sexy women so erotic, but the thought of me and another woman so disgusting?"

"I didn't say it was disgusting. It's disturbing, insulting. We are not a bisexual couple. Or are we? Joan, if this is some new phase, some problem, you'd better let me know." He was still talking to the ceiling.

"And?"

He remained deep in thought for a few moments.

"We'll work it out." He took in a deep breath and exhaled slowly. "I guess."

"Maybe I should speak to George."

"What!" He was up on his side, staring at me. "Why is it you women feel you can tell anything to anybody?"

"George isn't anybody; he's my friend."

"So then this *is* something, isn't it?" He looked as if he were going to be sick.

I didn't answer. I really didn't know. For the rest of the night I lay there going over the events of our lovemaking step by step. I liked when Manny entered me; it made me feel useful, but I rarely came at those times. The peak of my pleasure had little to do with the appendage he so valued. Women making love together excited him all right. I had watched enough X-rated videos with him to know that. So why not *his* wife? The answer had nothing to do with me or any other woman but in the very word *wife:* something that belonged to him and, therefore, was a part of him; something that he dare not let on to the world was less than perfect, lest it indicate any of his own sexual shortcomings. I closed my eyes and pictured Kate. I was undressing her again, sucking her nipples. I moved up to her face, but I could not kiss her on the lips. I just couldn't. I kissed her forehead, caressed the silky white hair. Her skin was translucent. Nikki's skin had been dark like mine, and her hair curly brown. Was this kissing inability my salvation, the confirmation that I was truly a man's woman? Or was I a denier? No matter. With my eyes shut and my ears deaf, left alone with my thoughts, there was no one in the world to take away my happiness.

Summer mornings were idyllic. I slept in a pair of shorts and a T-shirt so that I could stay in bed as long as possible and not have to spend time getting dressed before driving the kids to camp. Manny looked at me differently that day, as though some alien had come and invaded my body, and was mechanically occupying the place reserved for that woman his wife. We didn't speak. When he left for work, he said, "I'll see you tonight?" Half statement, half question. He had been thrown off center; everything was uncertain to him now.

I dropped the children off. Back home I stripped naked in front of the full length mirror. Although it was less than perfect, I liked what I saw. I touched myself: my breasts, my stomach, my genitals. Perhaps the devastation wrecked by age, childbearing, and a not so low in fat diet weren't the real reasons I had avoided studying my image for so many years. This female body of mine excited me. Masturbation, I reminded myself, was nothing new, and certainly not reserved for any particular sexual persuasion. I wanted to know if Mike Fitzpatrick had known about George's feelings. What if, at that tender age, George had tried to kiss Mike, and Mike had run away? It might have changed George's course for the rest of his life. And where the hell was Nikki Laperruta now anyway?

There were only two hours reserved for me alone that day before I had to pick up the kids: the kids, so little room in my life for change, and I was not thinking about time. I took a shower and got dressed. We would work it out Manny and I, just as he had said. We always did. And if he was having an affair? We would work that out too.

I walked towards town. In less than fifteen minutes, I was waiting at the crosswalk that lead to the florist. Some changes were mere detours; others smelled of chaos. It was there on the other side of the street, between La Belle Florist and Fred's Boot Shop, that I saw her.

"Kate," I called and waved, as I waited for the stoplight to turn green, the noonday traffic too heavy to jay walk. She looked around at first, trying to decipher where her name was coming from. I called out again, and she gazed across Main Street in my direction. It took a moment for her to recognize me, but she did.

"Hi!" she yelled, her mouth breaking into a smile. She had perfect white teeth.

"I got the knives," I shouted.

"Great! Did you cut yourself?"

"Yes!" I said, laughing. She laughed too. "And I'm still trying to stop the bleeding," she didn't hear me say as a bus pulled up in front of her with its screeching brakes and smelly exhaust. By the time the bus had taken off, she was gone.

FUTURE GAMES

Mommy giggles and whispers into the receiver. Although Sharon is only five years old, she knows Mommy is acting silly – different.

"Did you potty?" Mommy calls out, signalling that she has hung up and it is all right for Sharon to return to the kitchen.

"Yes," she fibs, flushing the toilet and taking naked Charlie, Mommy's hand-me-down Shirley Temple doll, off the new wooden rim of the hollow seat. There is no door to shut. It was the last thing Daddy had to do to refinish the bathroom, but when the summer began, he stopped working on anything in the house.

Sharon sits on the cool tile floor of the kitchen watching Mommy make *him* a birthday cake. Mommy is happy – singing.

"Do you love him more than Daddy?" Sharon asks, stirring an empty metal bowl with a wooden spoon.

"Of course not," Mommy answers too quickly.

"Can I make this cake?" Sharon points to a lavishly iced chocolate layer cake beside a conglomeration of ingredients on the cover of one of her story books.

"No." Mommy laughs. "We don't know how much of anything to put in."

"Yes, we do. We can tell." She begins counting the number of eggs pictured in a large bowl.

"Honey, you can't do it that way." Mommy is still

happy; Sharon is angry. Mommy's happy because *he* called.

"We *can* do it. We can make this one for Daddy!"

"I told you we can't!" Mommy's voice gets high like a note on her grandmother's violin.

"We can too."

"Hurry and get ready," Mommy orders. "The babysitter's waiting."

"Where's my white hat?" Sharon asks.

"You can't wear a woolen cap. It's too warm."

"I want it."

"What for?" Mommy is annoyed.

"To pull over my eyes so nobody can see me."

Sharon doesn't always have to go to the babysitter; sometimes Mommy takes her along. She says they're going shopping, but they never do. Mommy wears a new dress, high heels, and lots of perfume. At home Mommy wears jeans and a T-shirt. As soon as they get off the train in town, Mommy says, "Let's have something to eat." Sharon wants to go to Burger Square, but Mommy says she's taking her to a better place. They go to a fancy restaurant with a lot of old people all dressed up. Mommy takes a crumpled kleenex out of her bag, quickly licks it and rubs hard at the corners of Sharon's mouth.

"Keep still!" she urges as Sharon pulls away from the sweet-smelling tissue. It smells like the inside of Mommy's bag, like the new perfume, like Mommy.

"Do you have to take her all the time?" Mommy asks, checking to see if anyone has noticed the naked doll on Sharon's lap as though it were an uninvited guest.

"Yes." Sharon strokes the matted golden banana curls. "She's my baby."

Then *he* comes. He's dressed the way Daddy looks on holidays or when Grandpa died. Sharon sits slumped in her chair, building a mountain out of her food with a heavy silver fork. She doesn't like it; it's some kind of chicken – always chicken. She likes it barbecued, the way Daddy makes it. But this is mushy with a lot of white goo all over it. Mommy says it's the plainest thing they have. He tells Sharon she eats like a bird. She wants to tell him he smells of licorice, or is it the chicken?

After lunch, the three of them walk down the avenue until they get to a tall building with doors that open by themselves. Sharon counts sixteen layers of solid glass forming shiny black bands around the white cement.

"This is where I work," he says.

"He's a lawyer," Mommy says, smiling.

Sharon doesn't know what a lawyer is and she doesn't care. Daddy works in people's houses. He's a tile setter. When he comes home at night, his hands are caked with cement and grout. This man's hands are clean and smooth, so smooth, Sharon easily slips her hand out of his as he tries to pull her towards a balloon vender. Sharon loves balloons; she doesn't like *him*.

"He smells like licorice," she tells her mother as they ride the metro back to the suburbs. The train is hot and stuffy. Sharon's shoulders begin to ache as though the heat were weighing her down.

"It's tobacco. He smokes a pipe."

"It smells like licorice to me. I hate licorice."

"How would you like to go to the library?"

"Daddy doesn't smoke a pipe, does he?"

"No, Daddy doesn't smoke. Let's go to the library, okay?"

"I'm glad Daddy doesn't smoke. I hate licorice."

Sometimes Mommy takes Sharon to his apartment. The building has an elevator in it and there's a balcony that's higher than the whole city. They never stay very long. Mommy and he stand and hug, sometimes even kiss when they think Sharon isn't looking. Sharon watches them from the balcony where she's supposed to be playing. One day she dropped Charlie off the railing while she watched. He was holding Mommy so tightly Sharon thought he must be hurting her. Even though he went down and got the doll, Sharon could not stop crying. He took a music box from his dresser and gave it to her. He said it had once belonged to another little girl he knew. It was a wooden box with purple and white flowers painted on it. When Sharon lifted the lid, she was delighted with a pink ballerina that popped up and began twirling around while a strange tune played. She stopped crying. On the way home Mommy said, "Let's not tell Daddy about the music box. Let's not even tell him where we went today. Okay? It'll be our secret. Our little game." She always said this after they left his apartment, that it was their little secret, part of their little game.

On the way to the babysitter Sharon does not speak. She is wishing for September. In September, she will go to kindergarten. No more babysitters, no more lunches.

"Are you mad at me?" Mommy asks. Sharon shrugs her shoulders.

At the babysitter's she plays with Charlie as though it

were a chore, twisting her legs and arms every which way, making her sit or dance or run, torturing the doll by ripping out its limbs, then snapping them back into their sockets.

"Where are her clothes?" the babysitter asks.

"She doesn't have any."

"Would you like to make her some?"

"No! She doesn't have any!"

"Are you sad today?"

"Yes," Sharon says, scribbling with a pencil on the cover of her coloring book.

"What's wrong?"

"I don't know. *He* called Mommy today."

"Who called?"

"Nobody."

That afternoon, while Mommy is in the kitchen cleaning up the mess she made baking the birthday cake, Sharon goes into the desk drawer. She takes out a ballpoint pen and two felt-tipped markers – one blue and one red. Then she goes into the bathroom, climbs onto the toilet seat cover, reaches over to the counter and takes the round mirror with the gold stand that Mommy uses to put on her makeup. She gets down from the toilet seat with the mirror carefully held in two hands. Once she is steady on the floor, she picks up the pens she has left on the edge of the sink and carries everything into her bedroom.

She sits on the floor behind her white rocking chair and turns the mirror over to the magnifying side. With the blue marker, she draws two long lines on top of her eyebrows. Then she repeats this motion about ten times over each eye. Next, she fills in her lips with the red pen. She is just poking her cheek with the ballpoint pen to make two large beauty marks like Mommy's when Mommy walks into the room. Sharon comes out from behind the rocker smiling. Mommy screams her name and grabs her by the wrist. As she pulls her out of the room, Sharon feels her legs collapse under her and drag along the floor. Her wrists are burning and Mommy keeps yelling. If she would only stop yelling.

Mommy takes her into the bathroom and begins scrubbing Sharon's face with a washcloth. It's too hot and soap keeps getting in her open mouth because she's crying. Mommy is rubbing hard and still yelling. As she scrubs, the washcloth turns blue and red, then purple. Sharon keeps crying; her mother keeps yelling. When she's finished, Mommy asks why Sharon did it.

"I didn't take yours. I used my own." Sharon stares into the two fleshy cushions which seem to be swelling out of the top of Mommy's dress. She cannot look at her face.

"Why didn't you ask me?"

"Because I wanted to surprise Daddy. I thought you wouldn't let me. I wanted to be pretty for Daddy."

"You don't need to do that for Daddy; you're pretty enough," Mommy says.

"You do it for *him*."

"I don't do anything special for him! You hear? I don't do anything special for anybody!" Mommy shouts, her hands held high and shaking, the painted red tips flashing. Sharon winces thinking Mommy's going to hit her, but Mommy runs out of the room, leaving Sharon sitting on the toilet seat with soap on her face.

At night, Sharon takes the music box out of her drawer and brings it into the living room – partly because she wants to play with it; mostly because Mommy has been mean to her. Daddy doesn't notice it. Sharon winds it all the way and drops it on purpose. The ballerina appears, spinning on its side as the music plays at a fast tempo.

"Where did you get that?" Daddy asks.

"At *his* house."

While Sharon takes a bath, Mommy and Daddy argue.

"You know you're really something. You take *her* to *his* apartment. You're really something!" Daddy says.

Good, Sharon thinks. That'll teach her.

"She doesn't know what's going on," Mommy says.

"Like hell. She's probably listening right now."

"That's because you're talking so damn loud!"

"I'm telling you – she knows!"

"She's barely five."

"How naive can you be?" Daddy bangs his fist on the table.

"Okay. So maybe she knows something. Maybe she has figured it out. Maybe sometimes I just don't care."

Sharon is cold, so cold. She gets out of the tub, puts on her nightgown and runs into bed. Her bedroom is farther away, away from her parents, from the shouting.

"I'm warning you. This whole thing has gone way too far!" She can still hear her father say.

"Look, you agreed to this, remember? It was supposed to, quote, loosen me up a bit, make me more uninhibited. You're the one who said I needed it. 'Go ahead,' you said, 'maybe you'll learn something.'"

"I thought it would help things. I didn't know what else to do."

The words become an ugly chanting with no meaning to Sharon's ears. She buries her head in her pillow, suffocating Charlie with the weight of her tiny chest. Then a funny thing happens. Daddy comes into Sharon's room. The child is frightened and pretends to be sleeping. Suddenly she feels his sandpaper hand sweep her bangs to one side. She opens her eyes.

"Daddy, what's wrong?" Sharon begs for some explanation.

"Your mother is having an affair," he says, staring but not seeing her.

"What's an affair?"

As though he hasn't heard what he said or what she asked, he gets up and walks out of the room. The back door slams shut. Soon Mommy comes into her bed. She doesn't like when Mommy does this because her bed is too small and Sharon gets pinned against the wall while Mommy tosses and turns all night.

"Why can't you sleep with Daddy?" she asks.

"Go to sleep!"

"Is Daddy coming back?"

Mommy hugs her and pulls her closer to her shaking body. "Don't cry, Sweetheart. Be a big girl for Mommy. Don't cry." She isn't crying. It's Mommy who's crying.

Sharon wakes up in an empty bed. She is surprised at what she finds in her parents' room. They're both asleep, her father's arm around her mother's bare shoulders, her mother's head wedged in her father's armpit. Maybe the fighting is over. They'll go out to the Pancake House this morning. They'll have company for dinner. Daddy always wants to invite friends but Mommy says it's too much trouble. Then they fight.

Mommy and Daddy get out of bed without a word. Nobody looks at anyone. Nobody talks at breakfast.

That night, *he* comes to the house. Sharon has to stay in her room. She can't hear what they're saying too well because they keep their voices low. She can hear some things though like, "Enough . . . I don't want you seeing her anymore . . . Not your business . . . Damn . . . I love her." She isn't even sure who's saying what. Mommy's walking around the house sniffling. Whenever she comes into Sharon's room, Sharon pretends she's sleeping; she's praying for him to leave. Finally, the screen door opens and closes. He's gone.

Then Mommy and Daddy start talking. They get louder and louder. Mommy's crying. Mommy's always crying.

"I'll leave," she says.

"If you do, you don't take her! I'll take you to court. You know you don't have a chance."

"How can I go without her?"

"That's your problem. I've had it with the whole goddamn mess!"

"Stop! You're hurting me!"

Sharon pulls the quilt over her head. Her stomach feels tight, inside out. She mumbles over and over, "Stopitstopitstopitstopit," hoping somehow they will hear her. The screen door slams shut one last time. She knows it was Daddy. From the hallway, she sees Mommy leaning against the kitchen cabinet, rubbing her wrist, sobbing, her face wet, her nose running.

Sharon has been at Grandma's house for a week. Mommy said it was another game. She was visiting a friend in another city. Daddy said he had a lot of work to do. The weather is changing. It was so cold yesterday, Sharon had to wear a jacket outside while she played. It's quiet at Grandma's. It's such a big house and there's so much to do; but it's so quiet. Grandma bakes cookies with Sharon; she takes her to the park; she invites her next door neighbor's little boy to play. At night, Sharon sees Grandma staring beyond the TV, beyond the walls of the house.

"Are Mommy and Daddy coming back, Grandma?"

"Of course."

When Mommy walks into Grandma's house, she hardly looks at Grandma. She doesn't have any makeup on and she's wearing her glasses.

Grandma is mad.

"Wash your face before you go home," Grandma warns her. "Put some lipstick on and put in your contacts. You look awful."

"Leave me alone!" Mommy snaps.

At home, Sharon finds Daddy in the living room shoving logs into the wood-burning stove. He looks tired. Mommy makes Sharon some hot chocolate and keeps hugging her.

"Are you warm enough, Sweetheart?" she asks over and over again. "Did you have fun at Grandma's?"

"Would you like to go to the movies tomorrow?" Daddy asks three times. Then Mommy talks.

"I'm going away again for a little while. A little longer

this time. I need to be alone. You'll stay here with Daddy. What's happening between Daddy and me has nothing to do with you. We still love you very much. You're the most important thing to both of us."

"Nothing else matters," Daddy adds.

"You do understand, don't you, Sweetheart?" Mommy asks.

"I guess so." Sharon stares at the floor.

That night Sharon prepares to leave. She takes the red plaid overnight bag she has just brought home from Grandma's and dumps the dirty clothes onto the floor. She puts in her favorite stuffed bunny, her two lucky silver dollars, her elephant charm she found in the park, and her white cap. If she leaves, they won't fight over her. Mommy can stay and won't have to see *him* anymore. It's Sharon's turn to leave. After all, they're the most important things to her. She loves them more than anything. Then one day, when she's grown up, maybe ten, she'll come back and they'll be so happy to see her nothing else will matter. And everything will be the way it was a long time ago.

She picks up the music box and holds it for a moment, then hides it under her bed. She doesn't want to take it with her. She doesn't want Daddy to see it. She doesn't want Mommy to find it. As she places Charlie into the satchel, she becomes very tired. She climbs into bed. If only she were six, she thinks. Six is so big. Then she could go away. Sharon falls asleep fully clothed under the lavender quilt, her overnight bag on the edge of the bed.

THE TOOTH HEALER

I am driving to Great Barrington to see this so-called tooth healer only because it is easier than having to stare down into the dejected face of my patient, Jim Sheppard, next week, and in the middle of his root canal tell him that, once again, I did not go. I have all the information he gave me right here on the dashboard: some guy who turns amalgams into gold inlays and straightens teeth with a touch on one's shoulder – right.

Despite my skepticism, I have lived in New England long enough to know that the final temperate evenings of our short summers are to be relished, so I find this trip up to the Berkshires pleasant – the oldies station blasting, my singing along to no one's desired volume but my own.

"... *More than any time before this heart of mine seems to need you so much more. The touch of your lips, the thrill of your embrace keeps saying that no one could ever take your place* . . ."

Tonight Tonight – the Mello Kings! I haven't missed one yet. I can remember every word, all the artists as well as I could thirty-five years ago, holding a transistor radio to my ear at the corner schoolyard in Brooklyn.

I've taken my wife's car because if I stopped to get gas for my own, I'd be late. Last year, I never made it – left the directions home and got lost. Colleen keeps a stash of candy in the glove compartment, the kind of treat my grandmother used to have in a colored glass dish on top of her coffee table or at the bottom of her black leather pocketbook with the gold clasp, those hard suckers wrapped in the cellophane image of a slice of fruit. I'm enjoying a lemon one now, turning it around with my tongue to a different spot in my mouth after I've sucked long enough to let the tartness sting, and finally numb. Then I go for it, bite down hard on the remaining piece and sink my teeth into the sticky jelly center – the part I used to hate, the part I had forgotten about. Something always has to ruin a good thing. I open the window and spit it out.

I'll get home late tonight and Colleen will be asleep or feigning sleep. I'll begin to pet her, attempt to arouse her, but her stiffened body will tell me she is putting up with it and will be relieved when I have what she calls my *volcanic eruption* so she can roll over and slip back into her state of unconsciousness.

"You don't really want to do this?" I asked her last night.

"I'm doing it, aren't I?"

"Yes, but you don't really want to."

"Fine! Forget it!" She pulled the sheet up to cover most of her face, a lock of chestnut hair fell over the rest of it.

I've loved her for over sixteen years; she tolerates me. How long has it been like this? I've lost track. Most marriages get depressed from time to time, yet I'm not consoled by that fact. I play along: work my butt off, coach soccer, fund raise for the United Way; still I can't feel good about any of it. It's like playing tennis without a ball, like swimming in the sand.

"What's wrong with Ira?" I overheard a neighbor ask Colleen at a barbecue last weekend.

"Oh, he just hates his life right now."

Moody Ira, demanding Ira. Haven't you heard? Happiness is an illusion.

"So who's happy?" my mother would say as I, a ten year old, sat on the front stoop, brooding because my friends hadn't played stickball with the enthusiasm I anticipated, and afterwards, were content to simply move on to something else. But *I* wanted to celebrate it – not the victory, rather the comradery, the feeling.

Most of my patients complain about how their husbands hide behind newspapers, fade into television screens. My wife stalls each night: enzymes her contact lenses; fools with creams and lotions; sits up jotting down lines of creativity for her next poetry group, hoping all the while that I will be sound asleep when she finishes.

"Don't write about me," I've warned her.

"Don't worry, I'm not."

"Let's hug."

"Don't start, Ira. It's never just a hug. It's late. I can't stay up until one in the morning. I have the kids to deal with tomorrow. I have work."

"Don't let me beg, Colleen."

"You're like a child," she says.

Then I pick up the novel I've been reading three pages of each night and pause after every paragraph, glancing over to see if Colleen has fallen asleep. When she finally dozes off, I masturbate.

On my wedding day, my mother sniffled and sulked. As she and I stood together in the center of a deserted dance floor, all eyes nostalgically gazing upon us, the band playing *Sunrise Sunset*, she whispered in my ear that this was the worst day of her life.

"You always had to be different," she said. "Your brothers liked French toast swimming in syrup – you, you ate it bone dry!"

"An Ira should never marry a Colleen," my grandfather warned in his heavy Yiddish accent. It's like mixing tables and chairs."

The analogy might have been wrong, but I understood what the old man meant; when you're close to someone, have a real relationship with them, you can read their minds. I want Colleen to read my mind.

I don't know any happily married couples right now. Oh, they don't admit to it, but you can see it in their laughless conversations, their compulsion for crowds, their absence of touch. I want to love every night like the first six months of intimacy, then hug afterwards, savoring the before and after. My greatest sorrow is that I can never meet my wife again, never court her again, never marry her again. It's all behind me. I'm a romantic who wants to have a good time. That's all I've ever wanted in life – to have a good time. Yet I feel as though I'm throwing my life away, as though nothing of what I'm doing is really worthwhile. Every day I wipe tears, numb pain, clean out infections; still, I find no relief from the ache of listening to my own emotions.

THE TOOTH HEALER

The auditorium, a small wooden structure, is packed with two or three hundred believers of all ages. I sit at the end of a row in the back. As he enters, their expressions and applause make it clear that many have seen him before. He is big, hefty, and white, a man in his mid-seventies, a self-proclaimed reverend who received a calling to travel and to heal. To me, in his full snowy-white beard and ivory suit, he is Colonel Sanders selling snake oil.

The first thing he asks for is a ten dollar donation. A woman in her thirties, modestly dressed in a blouse and skirt, passes a basket up and down the aisles. I do not contribute to the overflowing green bills. I sense an incredible awareness in the woman who scans the faces of each one in the crowd as the basket comes around. There is something exciting under the prim, friendly appearance – something manipulative, wicked. Money collected, she approaches the stage and speaks in a captivating but doubtful southern droll; she is his wife. Her job is to prepare the audience for the Reverend Averill Hall by telling how she witnessed his greatness at a prayer meeting in Arkansas, and thus, came to stay with him.

Reverend Hall speaks now, his accent is richer, more convincing. He tells about his introduction to a healer of some kind, after which through "tacit" conversation with God, Hall, himself was shown how to heal. All the while, I cannot take my eyes off of his wife Olivia, who never moves from his side. She gazes adoringly upon him as if she knows what he is going to say, not because she has heard it a million times before, but because she reads his mind.

They proceed to section the room into three groups

that form lines. Hall, his wife, and a male helper stand at the head of each, and as the congregation passes by, they bestow a blessing by tapping once, ever so lightly, each person's left shoulder with their right hands. I have made sure to wind up on Olivia's line. When I approach her, I do not look into her face, but rather at her breasts, well-defined even behind the buttoned-down cotton blouse. She smells of fresh lilies, and I want to pin her hand onto my shoulder, wrap my arms around her small waist, and bury my head into her chest. I receive my blessing and return to my seat.

Colleen blames all of her dislikes about men on testosterone, and most of the world's ills on the fact that men are physically stronger than women. I can see the disdain in her expression when I encourage my three-year-old son to pee in the yard, instead of interrupting our baseball game and making him use the toilet. A primitive rite of passage of some cannibalistic tribe, she is thinking, relegating me to nothing above the ancestral ape. It is the same look she gives me when I pour mounds of Parmesan cheese on everything. Always overdoing it, she says. Never enough.

"Mommy, can a woman get pregnant from an animal?" my eight-year-old daughter asked one morning as Colleen stirred a cup of coffee.

"I guess so," Colleen answered, casting that same snide glance at me.

"You aren't happy," I told her later.

"No, *you* aren't happy."

"I'd just feel better if we made love more. When I don't have sex, I'm off-centered."

She took in a deep breath and exhaled quickly.

"Look, Ira. It's a mid-life crisis." She tried to mask her annoyance with compassion.

"How do you know? I've always wanted this. I don't see it as a mid-life crisis."

"*Everyone* has mid-life crises," she said, typically like her, speaking in absolutes, all or nothing.

"And what about you?" I inquired.

"I've been having one for two and a half years."

"You mean you haven't been happy for almost three years?"

"No, not really."

Colleen says I have an unrealistic attitude toward marriage, that it's impossible for two distinct psyches to function as one. All of our friends make bad jokes about their sex lives or lack of. It reminds me of the way my father and the other men at the Catskill bungalow colony where I spent my childhood summers lusted over the two Goldstein sisters, one blond and voluptuous, the other brunette and voluptuous. On Friday evenings, the men would come up, all hot and sweaty from their drive out of the city, and pant like puppies when they saw the Goldstein sisters' husbands embrace the tanned, halter-clad bodies. "Va va va voom!" the men would say, shaking one of their hands up and down like a Spanish woman fanning herself in a hot Madrid metro car. It would embarrass me, yet I, too, remember getting excited as I conjured up what the evening held in store for those gentlemen.

But sex isn't all I want from a marriage. I want it to be

something bigger than life, all-encompassing, I've explained to Colleen many times. She tells me *I* should have been the poet because *I'm* the dreamer. That's when I turn my ugly side to Colleen and sourly tell her how we have nothing in common, never did.

"We used to like music," she says defensively.

"Everyone was into music then."

"What about politics?"

"Everyone was into that then, too."

With that she cries herself to sleep, saying she doesn't understand me. The next day she is solicitous, comes tiptoeing around me, tries to engage me sexually, start over, but I won't let her. After awhile, she goes off angrily slamming cabinet doors and drawers, and I feel badly that I've hurt her, so badly I can't swallow, I can't cry, I can barely breathe, as though a cold lump of mashed potatoes were stuck, weighing heavily, somewhere between my lungs and my stomach.

"I wish you liked me," I tell her when we reconcile.

"I like you. *You* don't like *me*."

I've thought about this issue she often brings up, that it is actually *I* who am rejecting *her*. She's wrong; I've always been attracted to her. I see the way men look at her and I want to shake her up and say, you're still beautiful, a seductress – seduce me! But she is not talking about physical attraction. Do I like her? is the question, and not just because she's the mother of my children. She is convinced that if she fulfilled my desires, clung to me, I would crave the battle and turn away, leave. I don't want a divorce; Colleen takes good care of me. Why is it that I harp on what she does not do for me rather than what she does do? Besides, I'm too disorganized. I wouldn't remember which child was supposed to be with whom and when. And I've worked hard to arrive this far in my relationship; why would I want to start again with someone at point A?

Except for sex – yes, there I could start at A.

Reverend Hall continues to preach of his accomplishments: a man once came to the Reverend, complaining about the pain caused by his dentures; he could barely chew. Hall told him to have faith. The next time Hall saw the man, the miracle had already occurred; the discomfort had actually been caused by a new set of teeth that was growing under the dentures. The man was saved by his faith – and Hall, his only conduit. What a crock! We get two sets of teeth this time around and that's it. Yet the people cheer and Olivia beams. What must it be like to have someone so taken with you, so in love? I envision her removing her prim attire behind closed doors and coming alive solely for Hall, catering to his every whim and fantasy, still chaste in a sense, because she is devoted to him alone.

"You must take God in and let Him heal," Hall expounds.

Take me in, I can hear him say to Olivia. *Take me in*.

Olivia and the helpers hand out flashlights, and everyone busily looks into the mouths of others. It reminds me of going to Mass with Coleen on Easter Sunday, when the silence and occasional chanting is suddenly disrupted and the parishioners, with some awkwardness, frantically search for hands to shake while they whisper, "Peace be with you."

"Does anyone here have a particular request?" Hall asks.

The woman next to me, about twenty-five, emaciated looking, raises her frail, veiny hand and says she would like to have her front tooth straightened. She is homely, this fragile looking woman with dull brown hair pulled back into a ponytail, accentuating her exceptionally narrow jaw bone. Her eyes are large, sunken into their sockets and underlined with shadows. The thinness of her face even makes her slender nose seem too prominent. She is so needy-looking, so unhealthy compared to Olivia, who in a second is leaning over me, lending the woman her hand to guide her up to the stage. They both glance at me but only Olivia smiles, and I want to kiss her white neck in front of my face. The only thing crazier about the way I feel is Olivia's belief in Hall. At the podium, Hall shines a flashlight into the woman's mouth.

"It's beginnin' to straighten," he says, handing her a mirror, but she says she can't feel anything.

"It's early. Keep an eye on it n' have faith – it's gonna take a little while, child," he says matter-of-factly, then dismisses her as quickly as possible.

One man, an obvious plant in the audience, jumps up and says that he has seen Hall before and shown him a gaping hole in his mouth. Olivia ushers the man up and Hall peers into the anxious man's orifice.

"There's now a silver fillin' in the space," Hall proclaims. Not only that, but with faith and a few more visits to Hall, another hole in the man's mouth will also get filled. Olivia leads the congregation to applaud.

As I watch Olivia take the man back to his seat, I can feel her hand on his arm: warm, smooth, exciting. Her fingers are slender, her nails cut short, unpainted, unadulterated. Out of the blue, an old woman starts screaming, sobbing. She has a gold bridge in her mouth and hates it. She hates her parents for letting her have bad teeth. She hates her dentist for putting in the bridge. She knows her anger is irrational, but she can't help herself. She begins to shake; she's feeling that, as she speaks, the bridge is changing. The people sitting around her shine their flashlights into her mouth and agree – it is now silver. I can swear that the lighting in the auditorium is being altered. The woman approaches the podium; Hall puts a dental mirror into her mouth and confirms it. He tells her to keep having faith; just as the metal changed, so might it disappear. Others flock up to Hall and he shines a flashlight into each of their mouths.

"See, it's changin'," he tells them. "It's one color here and another color there."

The people cry hysterically. The fact that anything is changing is absurd, yet it has also moved Olivia to tears. I want to take her away, preferably to a motel, and save her from this charlatan. Hall invites people to come up and look into these mouths that have experienced change. I take him up on it. As I pass Olivia, I smile. She motions with her finger to come closer.

"Are you a dentist?" she asks.

Like a CIA agent who has blown his cover, I answer affirmatively and wish I were near an exit. Olivia smiles now; she thinks I, too, have been converted, so strong is her faith in Hall.

I search into the mouths of all these people claiming changes to be occurring, but I see none. When I shine the flashlight at one angle, because of the overhead lighting, the filling is brighter than usual; when I tilt the flashlight at another angle, the shine of the metal is normal.

Ludicrous. I quickly pass by Olivia again; this time fed up with her husband's bullshit, I wish her good luck and head for the door. I really want to say, "Come, let's drive to the Cape and roll around naked in the dunes. Let me rescue you. Forget this ass." But, instead, I relinquish my fantasy, and sink deeper into my own damn unhappiness. If she's foolish enough to believe in Hall, he can have her.

As I place my key in the car lock, I hear a woman crying, and I walk around the front of my car to find her standing at the driver's side of a gray sedan, her head buried in the crook of her elbow, resting above the door.

"Is anything wrong?" I ask startling her. She stares up at me. Only then do I recognize her as the painfully skinny young woman who had been sitting next to me before Hall abruptly dismissed her without providing more than faith for her crooked front tooth, and only then do I remember that she never returned to her place. "It can be fixed," I say. Her central incisor is certainly malpositioned. In fact, it is so twisted, it's perpendicular to her other teeth which are also crooked but not as bad. Petrified, she continues to gaze at me with those dark deep set eyes. "I'm sorry. I didn't mean to frighten you."

"Can it really?" she says, her sobs lessening.

"Oh yes. Someone must have told you that before. I mean a *real* dentist, not an idiot like him." I jerk my head towards the auditorium. She begins to cry again. I have insulted her judgment about coming to Hall in the first place.

"Hey, I was curious about him too. And I'm a dentist!" I lie about the curiosity part. It works. She smiles and I feel a bit of acceptance. "It wouldn't cost much to fix your tooth. Your family dentist could do it; you wouldn't even have to see an orthodontist."

"I haven't been to a dentist in nine years. My family stopped taking me when I was fifteen. They said it wasn't worth the money." She tries to inconspicuously wipe her runny nose with her hand. I remove a handkerchief from my pocket and hold it out to her, then think that maybe I should have pretended not to notice. However, she gratefully accepts the cloth and blows her nose.

"Have you tried to qualify for Medicaid?" I make a quick assumption about her financial predicament. She looks at me bewildered, as though trying to decipher what I am getting at, but then I see that her expression does not signify a lack of comprehension rather a request, a plea, for it is from me that she seeks understanding. It's of no use, her eyes tell me, can't you see that? It's deeper, much more.

"It doesn't matter, really, it doesn't. You're very pretty the way you are." She is not reassured. "You remind me of someone. An actress. I can't recall her name."

"Right." She breaks into a timid smile.

"You do." I grin at her. "Your eyes are lovely. Are they gray or brown? It's hard to tell in the dark." I lean closer to her.

"They're brown."

"Maybe it's a dancer you remind me of. A ballerina. I'm so bad with names."

She laughs, not believing me for a moment, enjoying the attention regardless. And it seems the more I feed this young woman with compliments, the more she laughs, and the more she laughs, the more I think that, here, in the absence of luminary trickery, the only lighting being that of the crescent moon, this woman really is quite attractive and, like me, so very lonely.

"It wouldn't bother you to kiss someone with a tooth

like mine?" She takes me by surprise, as she turns from me and stares out into the darkness.

"What would that have to do with it at all?"

"I don't believe you. You're like him." She points toward the shed. "You're just trying to convince me of something that isn't."

The thought of being compared to that quack incites me so, before I know it, I am leaning closer to her, taking her bird-like face into my left hand. With my wedding band pressing against her delicate Class 3 mandible, I gently position her towards me. I kiss her once, twice, then tilt my head to the side and, as she opens her mouth, we continue to kiss for, I don't really know – ten, fifteen, twenty minutes. No thought of Colleen, no pang of guilt breaks my concentration as we almost compete to devour one another. I wrap my arms around her skeletal frame which threatens to snap as I squeeze her tightly. Encircling my waist with her thin arms, we stand protecting each other from the pain of all the Halls, the Olivias, the parents, even the Colleens of our worlds.

"I have to go," she finally says, pulling away abruptly.

"Me too."

There are no questions asked, no phone numbers exchanged, no excuses made. She is not thoroughly convinced that what I have told her about being appealing to men is true despite what we have just engaged in, yet behind the troubled face I sense a contentment, perhaps equal to the warmth that radiates from within me, and at the moment I can see that she really is beautiful. Standing alone, I watch her pull out of the lot, as I listen to the crunching sound her tires make on the gravel.

The mountain air has chilled. I drive, anticipating a

heavy uneasiness to fill my stomach, like the certain sensation one has upon waking from a wet dream only to discover the provocation was unfounded, like finding the jelly in the center of the candy, like believing everything Colleen has ever said about me to be true. I anxiously wait, but it never comes.

I will not bother Colleen tonight. I will not pet her, paw at her, try to wake her. Maybe in the morning, she will want to hug.

SURPRISE

Renée pulled up to the curb beneath the departures sign for United Airlines. She and her husband Jared got out and walked around to the trunk where he removed his backpack. It was big and red with a metal frame, and she couldn't imagine it being any fun having it on her back while climbing a mountain. She couldn't imagine having it on her back at all. But Jared was the outdoors lover in the family, not she.

"Just a week," he reassured her.

She wasn't worried.

"I won't be able to call. No cell phones allowed, and we're camping every night."

"No calls," she confirmed.

He kissed her, but the backpack weighed him down so he didn't seem to have any energy left to embrace her. She certainly couldn't hug him with Mount Everest on his back.

She always envisioned goodbyes at the airport to be laden with passion, but theirs never were. It was business as usual. Not that she or Jared traveled much, but there were his conferences to attend and lectures to deliver, and she had gone, from time to time, to visit her parents in Minnesota when they were alive. When Jared did go away, it was never for more than two or three days, and since her daughter had lived home up until last fall, there had always been someone there in the house with her. Renée drove away and concentrated on the exit signs. She kept her eyes pealed for Interstate 91 North, as though she hadn't ever been to the airport before.

Perhaps she should have arranged her week better, made more dates other than with the hairdresser, the dentist, the radiology department for her mammogram. Maybe she should have gone away altogether – visited her son who was clerking for a law firm in Philadelphia or her daughter who was trying to land an acting role in Hollywood. She had been busy at the library working overtime, filling in for a co-worker who was recovering from surgery; she hadn't spent much time thinking about her week alone. Alone. She had never lived alone but opted for roommates. She had never even spent a night alone except for one time when she was in graduate school at the University of Maryland getting her Masters degree in library science. All of her housemates had vacated one Friday night, leaving her to jump at any footstep or loud voices outside of the Hyattsville apartment. She remembers having taken hours to fall asleep (a kitchen knife under her pillow) and thanking God when daylight filtered through the curtains and found her in one piece.

The drive back to her house in Old Wyck took a long time. It took a long time to go anywhere from Old Wyck because Old Wyck was nowhere. Once she drove through the city of Redmont, it was one long and curvy two-lane road uphill to the eighteenth century white colonial that they had begun to renovate twenty-five years ago when Jared first was offered the position in the history department at the university in Redmont. She had been eager then to paint and hunt for cheap furniture – to please him. She hadn't minded living isolated on thirty acres of a former sheep farm at first. There were the children – three and two months old – to keep her busy, and the sanding and patching, and wallpapering. She had used power tools she had never known existed. But before long, the car became her homestead as she drove the children to school and every activity that Old Wyck just didn't provide and to the private school they attended because Jared didn't consider the regional school good enough. Then came her part-time job at the public library in Redmont: there was no library in Old Wyck. There were times she spent four hours a day in the car. It was more exhausting getting in and out, coming and going, than if she had driven straight through to New York or Boston. She began to wish for smooth linoleum floors that didn't leave splinters in her feet the way the wide pine ones did or whose nails didn't keep popping up no matter how many time she hammered them down. She began to wish for sirens and cars honking instead of owls hooting, or else dead silence. Jared, however, was content with his little estate; Jared spent the better part of his days at the university in Redmont.

When she finally entered her long driveway, it was dusk. She liked this time of day no matter where she was. In winter, everything was ice-blue and mysterious. In early summer, like now, a pink hue painted the landscape. She lingered in the car for a while looking at the mountains in the distance – purple and fuchsia in the evening light – but she was hungry and soon went into the house to fix herself something to eat.

She put tuna onto a defrosted bagel, topped it with some cheddar cheese, and placed it into the toaster oven. When female friends of theirs went out of town, Renée invited the men over for dinner. In fact, so many neighbors wined and dined them that it was difficult for them to find a free evening to come over at all. No one ever invited the women who were left alone, as though having to feed oneself were the only obstacle to overcome in being left alone. She washed her plate and cup. Zap! The sink was as clean as she had found it. When the children had lived at home, there were always dishes in the sink. She thought it would get better after they moved out and came home to visit, but it only worsened: they had been messy occupants attempting to fend for themselves; they returned messy guests eager to be waited on. She also learned that it had only partially been their fault since Jared never managed to get the dishes from the sink to the diswasher either, and handwashing was not in his vocabulary.

She fell asleep with the television on, every room lit up as though a party were going on. Seven nights by herself, and before she knew it, Jared would be back from Glacier National Park and his reunion hiking trip with his college buddies.

It was early Sunday morning when Renée awoke. She brushed her teeth, but before she went into the shower, she took Jared's toothbrush, razor, along with his comb lying on the side of the pedestal sink and placed them in rhe medicine cabinet. She washed down the shelf; she wiped away the dark whiskers and coils of gray hair from the basin. After she had showered, she took his dandruff shampoo from the wire rack hanging from the shower spout and put that into the medicine cabinet too. She got dressed. She picked all of Jared's dirty socks and underwear off the floor and put them into the washing machine in the laundry room next to their bathroom. She put his shoes into his closet. She pulled the sheets off the bed and threw them along with Jared's scent into the washing machine. She picked up all the journals he kept by his bedside, tied them into a bundle with string, and brought them to the basement. She attempted to tidy his dresser and wound up putting everything into a shoe box and brought that into the basement also. Wouldn't Jared be surprised how she had managed to clear away the junk he couldn't manage to sift through himself. She was making his life simpler – less complicated. She attacked his closet, pulling out shirts and pants and sports jackets and throwing them onto the floor. There were clothes he had worn before they were married. Poor Jared, he couldn't part with anything, not a pair of bell bottoms, not even the envelope a greeting card came in, or the reminder for an appointment that had long ago come and gone. Perhaps that's why he was a medievalist – he couldn't let go of the past. When there were but a few pieces of apparel left hanging in his wardrobe, she decided to take them out along with everything else. Wouldn't it be so much easier for him to start from scratch? Choose a few favorites and purchase a limited amount of new clothing? She found a large old air conditioner box in the basement and filled it with his belongings. She brought them to the attic so they wouldn't mildew. She spent the day this way: washing every item of clothing in the hamper, weeding through her own closet, packing away Jared's life, paring down her own. She was so exhausted by nightfall, she fell asleep in the dark.

She awoke late Sunday morning, undisturbed by the sunlight. She marvelled at how she had barely mussed up the bed linens: she was a light sleeper, and had only to smooth the sheets and comforter on her side of the bed, fluff up the pillow, and replace the sham she had moved onto Jared's side. When Jared slept, everything was so undone that she had to remove the top sheet (and blanket in winter) and comforter and begin from scratch, stretching across the king sized bed and walking around it several times to make it.

In the bathroom, she remembered the time she discovered a prophylactic in Jared's shaving case after he'd returned from a conference in California. He had denied any indiscretion – said it had been there for years before she'd had her tubes tied. She hadn't believed him, but she had forgiven him: everyone deserves a second chance.

She moved Jared's toiletries from the medicine cabinet, where she had placed them the day before, to the bathroom that the children once used.

She passed Jared's office on her way to the kitchen and shut the door. Too much clutter. She wasn't sure why he needed an entire room in the house when he already had an office at the university. He had found her in his study at home years ago, typing on his old IBM. She was writing a short story based on some family history (her great-grandmother had been a servant in Russia who managed to get pregnant by the son of her employer; they had fled to America). There was not enough room in the office for the two of them, Jared had said. Besides, she might misplace something – a student's exam, one of his lectures. She never wrote another word. She never stepped foot into his room again. Consequently, it was presently coated with dust. Served him right. It wasn't the space that had bothered Jared: he didn't like the thought of anyone creating. He approved of their son being a lawyer, but he frowned on their daughter's desire to act. She had a degree in theater and she should teach, he maintained. Renée understood perfectly well her daughter's desire to create; after all, Renée devoted a good part of her life caring for books written by *other* people.

Renée had intended to spend time in the garden, but she couldn't make it past the mudroom. Ski boots, poles, goggles, basketball sneakers, sandals, tennis balls and several racquets, work gloves, a baseball mitt, a bicycle pump. She took them all out to the barn. She spent the better part of the day vacuuming the entire house, mopping the floors, scrubbing the cabinets. She had to have it all in place and smelling of Murphy's Oil Soap and bleach before she could begin a project.

She didn't work on Mondays and Fridays, so she scheduled her appointments on those days. After her mammogram at the hospital in Redmont, she sank into the leather chair at her beauty salon. Her Venezuelan hairdresser Alfonso seemed to loom over her from behind like a scavenger about to seize its prey. In reality, he was shorter than she and so slight she often felt that if she shook his hand, he would wind up on the floor.

"What are we doing today?" he asked in his thick accent which she sometimes had trouble understanding. He liked to hum "Yellow Brick Road" and referred to Elton John as El Tunjun.

"What do you think?" She always answered.

"Clean it up a little, condition it," he said, examining the frizzy light brown ends flecked with gray that slipped through his fingers. Turning the hair under with cupped hands, he indicated the usual length around her chin line.

"Cut it," she said.

He shook his head with skepticism.

"It wouldn't look good?"

"*Sí*. It would look very good for me. But I have doubt that you are ready."

"You've been saying that for eleven years. Cut it. And change the color."

"No." He flatly refused.

"Then lighten it up. I want to see something different when I look into the mirror."

He nodded, as though suddenly understanding the secrets of the Taj Mahal, and began to hum.

She left the salon looking like Meg Ryan's mother – her head buoyant with the silvery blond wisps falling every which way. Her walk took on a bounce.

She loved Redmont. It was a small city – thirty thousand – but bustling: partly because of the university, partly because of many artists and transplanted New Yorkers who had taken up residence there. She thought about going over to the art museum at the university: she hadn't been there in years. She liked to avoid the university and meeting Jared, who was inevitably accosted by overeager coeds who questioned him about their term papers or the fascinating point he had made in The Social History of European Monasticism. Jared would go on in his sophistic manner while wide-eyed students, especially women, hung on his every word. The only thing Renée had ever found interesting about the Middle Ages was Monty Python. She decided against the museum and the likelihood of running into a colleague of Jared's (one up for review who felt he or she had to spend even summer days on campus) and forsook a conversation about Jared's ambitious mountain trip for lunch at her favorite French Restaurant. As she waited for a heaping spoonful of onion soup and sizzling cheese to cool, she gazed over the blue cafe curtains hanging from a thick brass rod in the window beside her and studied a row of three houses adjacent to the park. They had always appealed to her. Small, pinkish-beige stucco homes with flat fronts and steeply pitched moss-covered roofs, teal or green or black shutters, lace curtains, and geraniums and pansies cascading from window boxes. Set almost in the park itself, they could be a farmhouse in the French countryside or a cottage in the Cotswolds. Who lived in them? They were too small for a family. A spinster professor perhaps; a widow who had long ago emigrated with her husband from Provence. They must have been built to relieve the homesickness of that French lady. Renée spooned up the last drop of soup and scraped the crusted cheese from the rim of the bowl. She ate her salad.

On her way to work on Tuesday something red and black caught her eye as she took her usual route past the park. She drove around the block and passed by a second time. There on the front lawn of the middle cottage was a *For Sale* sign. She had been dying to get inside one of those homes for years. When she got to the library, she called the Realtor and made an appointment to see the house on her lunch hour.

It was in good condition. There was a small kitchen and eating area, a living room with a fireplace, and two bedrooms and a bath upstairs. The appliances were old, but the cabinets were in fine shape. Renée would have painted them blue. She liked the floral wallpaper in one of the bedrooms, and the other one was painted white – the whole house was painted white. She liked that. A clean palette. She would have added a little color here and there. She loved the narrow atrium doors that led out to a brick patio surrounded by giant rhododendrons in bloom. Deep purple clematis wound its way up a trellis in the corner, and red roses crowned a metal arbor.

"I didn't notice the sign yesterday," Renée told the Realtor Sally Boggs.

"It just went on the market this morning. But it won't last long. These houses never go up for sale. They're desirable being right by the park."

"How much are they asking?"

"One-seventy-nine nine."

"That seems like a lot for such a small house."

"It's a bargain. You have to remember that it's in Redmont for one. And then there's the park."

"How about one-fifty?"

"They do want to get it sold as soon as possible. The owner died. It belongs to her children who live out of town. But one-fifty – I don't know. I'll see what I can do."

"Try hard."

"Leave me your number. I'll phone as soon as I can get through to them."

Renée didn't believe her.

"What if someone else makes an offer before you reach them?"

"If it's higher than yours, I guess you're out of luck."

Renée wanted to give them the asking price, but she couldn't. She had a substantial amount of her father's inheritance in a savings account. Jared had wanted her to invest it all, but she had resisted, feeling securer with having some of it easily accessible.

"Offer them one-fifty cash."

Sally Boggs lit up.

"Well, that certainly might help matters. So many people have trouble with financing."

"Call me at Stoddard Library as soon as you hear."

It was a quarter past three when Sally Boggs phoned.

"They accepted. If you'd like to come by our office on your way home from work and sign a P & S, you've got yourself a new house."

"Sign a what?"

"Purchase and sale agreement."

"Right."

She did have herself a new house. Funny. She had never come close to buying anything like that on her own before. She felt great. It would be a little pied-à-terre. Her getaway. Jared would understand. After all, he had the university. No more long commutes. She could add on some hours at the library. Better yet, she could enjoy some long days in the city. See some plays.

That evening she phoned her friend Barbara who was an attorney: she didn't want to use their family lawyer.

"How soon can I get in?" she asked Barbara, who was rather stunned.

"If their lawyer already has the certificate of title and sends it to me along with writing the title insurance, we can close in a few days."

"You're kidding."

"I kid you not. Listen, Renée, are you sure you want to do this without Jared? Maybe you'd like to have lunch tomorrow. I can meet you at –"

"I'm sure, Barb. I want this house. But I'd love to have lunch with you anyway."

For years she had noticed a house about three miles

down the road, because in the driveway there was a beat-up gray vehicle with *Two guys and a big truck – You call us, we'll haul it* painted across the side. She had even memorized the phone number. One of the *guys* said he could squeeze her in on Friday.

On Wednesday and Thursday, she decided what she would take to the new house. The wicker furniture in the sun room for her new living room. The sofa bed in the family room so that the children would have a place to sleep since she was making the second bedroom her office. The oak drop-leaf table in the hallway would serve her well in her new dining area which was rather small. She took four of the dining room chairs, leaving the remaining four looking pathetic around a seven-and-a-half-foot table. She couldn't seem to eliminate many of the kitchen utensils: she loved to cook. She left several place settings in the cutlery drawer and the blender not to make it appear as though she had taken all of the small appliances. She would have taken the ironing board, but it was attached to the wall and concealed in a cabinet. She had lots of dishes and took only the good china and one set of blue English stoneware. She would leave the crystal that her mother-in-law had given them, which she always hated, and buy some colored stemware in the housewares section of TJ Max. She selected the brass bed and Victorian dresser and nightstand from the spare room, which she preferred to her own bedroom set. She had to have the oriental rug in the living room: she had bargained fiercely for it from a rug dealer in Boston. And the landscape her mother had painted, from over the fireplace. She took odd pieces from different rooms in the house with which to furnish her new office – a bookcase from here, a chair from there. She would buy all new sheets and towels.

She met Barbara at the closing in Redmont on Friday morning, after her dentist appointment. "Still on Cummings Road?" the dental receptionist had perfunctorily asked. For twenty-five years, she had answered to every front-desk person that everything was the same. Today she said no, and gave her new address. The young girl crossed out the old information and jotted down the new without giving it a second thought.

Nobody took any objection with the terms of the contract: the sellers weren't even present at the closing – just their lawyer and Sally Boggs. In thirty minutes, the house belonged to Renée, and by seven o'clock in the evening, she was all moved in. It was only then that she began to have second thoughts, but her cold feet had already been submerged into the icy waters. She could probably sell the house as quickly as she had bought it. These cottages were desirable, Sally Boggs had said. But who would act as impulsively as she had? She made up her twin bed and climbed into it. Her stomach muscles contracted into one massive knot. She would call Sally Boggs in the morning; she had made a terrible mistake. The passing traffic lulled her to sleep. An occasional honking of a horn woke her, but this she could get accustomed to.

It was late morning when she carried her breakfast out to the patio and ate on the wrought iron café set she had brought from the old house at the last minute, along with a wicker chaise lounge. She had left the monstrous gas grill for Jared: she would purchase a hibachi.

By the time she finished reading the newspaper and making her list of things to do for the week – movies to see, tag sales to attend, friends to notify of her new residence – it was three in the afternoon. Jared's plane was landing in two hours: it would take her almost that long to get to the airport. More if there was traffic, or an accident, or a breakdown. She leafed through the yellow pages and phoned a limousine service to meet him at the gate. Wouldn't he be surprised?

MAKING THE WINE

Angelo is in the bathroom shaving. I can hear him singing *uno stornello,* belting out the same stanza over and over again in his deep robust voice just the way he used to back in Italy. It is the only tune he ever bothered to learn at all. Soon he will come into the kitchen for his orange and cup of black coffee. Peeling the rind in a circular fashion as though he were carving one of his fine pieces of wood. Then, holding out a slice with the same hand that is still gripping the sharp paring knife, he'll say, "Caterina, take some. It's good for you."

I try to steady my hand as I lift the cup of coffee to my lips. Steady. Steady. Ah! I have spilled some on the table and Sophie must help me put the cup down. She wipes the table – her clean table. Now, Tom, Sophie's husband, has that look on his face as he sits across from me. He always looks like that when I spill something, or eat with my hands, or – almost all the time. I want to say to him, wait, you have no idea what it's like. You can't walk, you can't work, you can hardly think. But all I can manage are the same words each time: "I'm sorry." He gets up and walks out of the room.

Angelo is putting on his lumber jacket and going out to the garden. I tell him that I would go with him but my legs are very swollen. I have not been to the garden in years. Angelo goes religiously every day. He plants and weeds and keeps the rows of tomatoes, beans, eggplant, and squash neat like church pews. Then, at the end of the season, we can five hundred jars of tomatoes for Sunday gravy. Angelo has to have his pasta on Sunday. He loves to wake up to the aroma of his tomatoes seasoned with sweet *basilico* simmering for hours in the thick red sauce. When the children were young, they used to come home from church and dip chunks of thick-crusted bread in the bubbling hot gravy. "It's not done yet!" I warned them, but they loved it anyway. Then it was the grandchildren. They would walk over on Sunday mornings after church and do the same.

I never went to church. I wish I had. I made sure the children went, though. Children need religion, I used to think. But now I see it is old people who need it. Sophie won't take me. She says the Mass is too long and I will have to go to the bathroom. Once she brought the priest here to hear my confession. It was the third time I had confessed in my life. There was my First Holy Communion in Italy, all of us dressed like little brides. The second time was fifty years later. I don't know what possessed, but I wanted to go. Angelo laughed at me. He said I had nothing to confess. He said priests did not deserve to hear anyone's sins. When I came home from Saint Rosalie's, I told Angelo all about it, how I said it had been fifty years since my last confession, and he cursed and called me a fool.

Angelo taught me everything about life. I married him when I was almost sixteen; I didn't know anything. I didn't want to marry him but my parents made me. He was really very kind; with so much blond hair, blue eyes and a

Roman nose, my sisters thought he was wonderful. I thought he was too short. I didn't like any men; all I wanted to do was sit in a corner of the kitchen and read books. When Angelo came calling, I would pretend I was tired and go to bed. But he was so gentle, he took me to America and taught me everything. He told me there were diseases that people could get from making love. He knew because one of his *paisani* had gotten sick from a town whore. She had wanted Angelo to make love with her but he wouldn't. He is so smart, my Angelo.

Angelo is always hugging me and every night he wants to have a love affair with me. I don't like it so much. I'm tired at night and the heaviness of his body on my chest is suffocating. Sometimes I think he will crush my lungs. And it's messy; he spoils my clean sheets. Angelo is disappointed, but I just don't like it. But there was one time. I don't like to think about it, Angelo was so angry. Father Cioffi had come to visit right after the twin died. Angelo was at the barber's. The baby was only six months old then, and Father Cioffi kept bouncing him onto our bed, then lifting him high into the air and down onto the bed again. When Angelo saw the rumpled bedspread and the priest's black shirt pulled partly out of this black pants, he was furious. He ordered him to leave without an explanation; then he called me *putana*. "Whore," he said.

I cried and explained that nothing had happened, but he left the apartment cursing – always cursing. I was already in bed when he returned. He undressed quickly and began stroking my hair. When he climbed on top of me and pulled up my nightgown, I didn't mind, I was thinking of Father Cioffi, what it would be like, his tall strong body, his curly brown hair.

I think I will wash the dishes for Sophie. I want to, but where is the soap? I know it's here on the sink. Is this it? No, that's Sophie's china ashtray. Now, she's grabbing it out of my hands. "I only wanted to wash the dishes," I tell her. "Just sit down, Mamma," she says. "Just sit down."

Angelo will be coming in for lunch soon. He will want a plate of escarole, a piece of fresh Italian bread, and a large glass of red wine. I hope Sophie has remembered to fill the small bottle with wine from the basement. "How is the garden?" I ask him, as he comes to the door. "It will be a good garden this year, Boss." Boss. He has called me that forever. I do tell him what to do often. Maybe sometimes too much. But he needs it; he is too easygoing. There are things to be done. *Sempre si lavora*, one always works! Angelo likes to drink wine and laugh with people. His laugh is high pitched, almost hysterical. He does everything totally. I don't laugh too much. I have to work. Work is important. You can't have anything without working. Do you think we would have this land if I had not saved all our money? Oh, Angelo worked too, six sometimes seven days a week in the lumber yard, but he never made much money. Every night, he came home with splinters and he and Sophie would sit by the coal stove under the kitchen light. Sophie would take an embroidery needle she had sterilized with the flame of a match and poke at his callused hand while he screamed. He is very strong, Angelo; but if he is hurt, he cries out a lot just like a baby. Like when he has attacks of the gout and hollers when I walk into the room because vibrations make the sheet touch his foot. I stay awake all those nights. I want to sleep on the couch, to get some rest. I have to work the next day. But Angelo will not let me. He says I have to sleep with him in his bed every night. I am his wife.

I think I will put some coffee on for Angelo. Just turn on the gas. There. It will be done soon.

"Mamma, what are you doing!"

"What are *you* doing?" Damn you, Sophie! You are always taking things away from me. Damn you! I'll slap you! Again! Again!

"This is an electric coffee pot, Mamma. You've ruined it!"

But I never use an electric coffee pot. Angelo likes me to use the drip maker for his espresso. I keep it warm over the flame just before I pour it into his favorite demitasse. Then he puts in a few drops of *anisetta* and a twist of lemon rind. I never use an electric pot. And that man sitting across the kitchen table keeps staring at me with that look again.

"Sophie, who is that man?"

"It's Tom, Mamma."

"Why don't you let go of my hand? Sophie, you're hurting my hand!"

It's time for the radio now. After lunch, Angelo likes to listen to the news and then the stock market report. We don't own many stocks, just a few of AT&T, but Angelo likes to know what's going on. I don't understand it very much. Still, if it weren't for me, Angelo would never have been able to buy those stocks. I work hard, day after day, in the machine shop sewing clothes. Even though Angelo is retired, I still work, and he drives me to the factory in town every morning and picks me up each evening. I look out of the fourth story window and see him sitting in the old black Dodge. He is always there twenty minutes before quitting time. He is never late.

But Angelo spends too much money. Like the time he bought a sixty-dollar typewriter for Sophie during the Depression, and in cash! He could not turn away the young salesman standing in the doorway of our apartment. Or the time he bought me the diamond brooch for our fiftieth wedding anniversary. I was angry. He should not have ordered a custom-made brooch from Italy. I scolded him for spending so much money. And I showed him. I never wore it until the day he died; since then I have never taken it off.

Angelo is going outside now to work on the trellis he is building for my roses. He knows how much I love flowers. "Be careful," I tell him.

"Don't worry, Boss," he laughs.

"And the grape arbor, don't forget to fix the grape arbor!"

Every year Angelo and I make gallons and gallons of wine. The last time we made the wine it happened. I knew I shouldn't have made it. I felt the pressure mounting in my chest. It was getting hard to breathe. But we had to make the wine. If we didn't, the grapes would go bad. All that time and money would be wasted. We had to make the wine and we did. And it happened. My heart. I remember the first time I opened my eyes after the attack. Angelo was standing over my hospital bed like a frightened schoolboy on his first day of class. Suddenly, he threw himself across my still body and wept even harder than when the baby died, harder than I had ever seen him before. I took his hands in mine and held it as tightly as I could. "Don't cry, Angelo," I said. "I made it. Didn't I?" He nodded. "I made the wine, Angelo. I made it."

Angelo loves living here in the country. It reminds him of our *paese* in the mountains of Rome. Thanks to me, we were able to save the money to buy it. I used to cook cheap meals and sew the children's clothes so we could save. And little by little, we saved enough to buy a few acres, then a few more. And we never owed anybody – nobody. Angelo is different here with the grandchildren. In the city he was mean and strict with our children. He was afraid for them – this new country with all of its freedom. There were so many things to get in trouble with: gangsters, cars, subways. If the children were not home on time, he would go out looking for them. And then, when he got them home, he would send them from one side of the parlor to the other with a single slap. But here in the country, he plays with the children, chasing them around the farm with his belt folded in half and snapping it, pretending he will catch their fingers in it if they dare to stick them in. But we are not in the country anymore, are we? And work? I can barely lift myself from this chair which has become a part of me, an extension of myself.

"I have to go to the bathroom again," I tell Sophie.

"It's too late, Mamma. Look what you've done!"

I don't remember doing it. One minute I had to go to the bathroom and the next minute I called Sophie. Maybe it wasn't the next minute. Maybe it was a long time after. Is that possible? I keep looking at Sophie, waiting for her to tell me if it was a long time after.

It is almost four o'clock. I have to turn on the television because Angelo will be in soon and he'll want to watch our story. This and wrestling are the only programs he loves. When he watches wrestling, he howls and squeals as though he was right there in the audience. Oh, and *Gunsmoke*, he loves to watch *Gunsmoke*. But our story is his favorite. It's on every day and is about a nice girl named Nicole. Nicole has a lot of problems. Right now, she's pregnant but can't find the father of the baby, who really loves her, but doesn't know she's pregnant. Every afternoon, we watch to see what Nicole will do. I hope Sophie is making stuffed peppers and sausage for dinner. Angelo likes to eat stuffed peppers and sausage on Monday nights. I think I smell sausage.

After dinner, Sophie gives me a bath. I wish I could bathe myself, but I can't seem to remember what to do. I get into the tub, and I'm fine. I go for the soap, and I get confused. I get so confused. Then my head begins to hurt, and I am dizzy. I'm afraid I will fall. But I'm sitting. My head hurts so much.

"Sophie, it hurts."

"What hurts, Mamma?"

"I don't know."

I always fell good after my bath, but I never want to take one. Sophie tells me it's good for me, but I'm afraid. Tom tells me I'm dirty and smell. I never know what will happen to me there in all that water. I don't care if I smell. I'm afraid.

Yesterday, or maybe it was last week, Sophie took me to a nursing home. It wasn't really a nursing home but something better. The floors were very shiny and it smelled like a hospital. There were groups of people sitting in wheel chairs singing old songs. They looked so cold. I like to sing.

We sat in an office, and a man behind a desk asked me a lot of questions. I knew I had five children, but I couldn't remember any of their names, just Sophie's. I couldn't remember one other name.

"She knows the words to old songs," Sophie said right away.

"Fine, then, let's hear one," the man said.

So I started singing "Ramona," But when I looked at Sophie, she was crying, without a sound, just tears streaming down her face. Don't cry, Sophie, I can remember the words. Don't worry, I thought, I know the words.

Then a funny thing happened. The man said "no" to Sophie. He said I didn't qualify. And Sophie helped me out, and she was smiling.

Tomorrow is the anniversary of Angelo's death, and I want Sophie to take me to church to the Mass they will say for him. Angelo never went to church after the time with Father Cioffi, but they will say a Mass for him anyway. I didn't tell the priest he never went to church. He should have gone; we both should have gone.

I sleep with Angelo tonight as I have for all these years. He snores loudly and rhythmically to the noisy ticking of the alarm clock on the night table. I have never known any other man in this way except him. I want to have a love affair with you tonight, Angelo. What? No, I cannot promise I will like it, but I won't complain. Angelo, can we have a love affair tonight?

AFTER VICTORY

Her husband Rocco sulks all morning. Barely touches his soft-boiled egg. Leaves an almost full cup of coffee. Yet Vicky will let nothing dissuade her.

Vicky spent much of the night awake, planning her attire: a blue linen suit and a white crepe V-neck blouse with a string of pearls. No, it's August, too hot for a suit. Besides, the linen would wrinkle during the ride. She chose a floral two-piece sleeveless dress with a scarf that ties at the throat (to hide her slightly sagging neck) and a blouson top to cover her rear end.

It's fuchsia and white, perky and uplifting – not like funeral garb.

"Have some." Vicky hands her daughter Toni a plate of French toast before her second foot crosses the threshold. "I have fresh coffee."

"I thought we'd have lunch in Castleton," Toni says.

"That's a long way from now."

"If I eat this, I won't be hungry later."

"So lunch will cost less."

Toni sits at the kitchen table and eats her French toast, while Vicky picks out a cardigan to take along: she hates air conditioning. She wants to ask Toni's opinion, but doesn't want to make a big deal of it in front of Rocco, who has retired to the den. She selects her white cotton knit and runs into the bathroom to check her hair. She thanks God that she colored it last week. She grabs a compact and dark pink lipstick from the vanity drawer. She wishes she had been able to sleep last night: tiredness is an elderly woman's nemesis.

"You want one?" Vicky now offers Toni an opened jar of cherries soaked in vodka, which she made last summer.

"It's nine in the morning!"

Vicky shrugs her shoulders indicating the hour is irrelevant. She stabs two cherries with a fork and pops them into her mouth. The juice burns the inside of her cheeks as she bites down and chews; she swallows and lets the alcohol warm her insides – fortify her. She is on her way to meet Andrew Lingua, her love of fifty years ago.

"We'll be back around three," Vicky calls to Rocco who is watching a rerun of *Bewitched*.

"I think this is absurd," he bellows.

"I don't care what your think," she mutters under her breath.

"You'll probably get lost," he calls after her.

It was around Thanksgiving when Andrew's first call threw Vicky DiBenedetto's life off balance. She was at the kitchen table doing the crossword puzzle. Rocco was in the den, watching *Wheel of Fortune* on TV.

Vicky had already washed two dishes, two forks, two knives, and two glasses, scrubbed the pots, and wiped down the table and stove top. Lamb chops. She remembers. She broiled loin lamb chops: seven ninety-nine a pound at the Big Y Supermarket, buy one pound, get another free that week. They had eaten at five o'clock as they always do. There was a time, however, when they still lived in Brooklyn and they were young, that they ate at seven or seven-thirty. That's what her husband had been used to growing up in Sicily. That was the civilized European hour to dine, he always said; however, Vicky knew Rocco really preferred it because he didn't want too much free time left over before he retired for the evening. After dinner, there was half an hour of television, maybe an hour if *Bonanza* was on, and he was off to bed so that he could rise at four in the morning and set out for the Italian bread bakery that he owned.

In those days, their severely handicapped daughter Susan (whom they later placed in a nursing home with pediatric long-term care) was already in bed by the time he got home. That was what he counted on. Nevertheless, there were those difficult nights, particularly in her early years, when her wailing disrupted their meal and it sometimes took the two of them to calm her down and get her to bed. There was no TV on those occasions. Rocco would just close the door to their room, strip down to his shorts and undershirt, and go to sleep.

Nowadays, they can hardly wait to eat supper; their entire day revolves around it. From the moment Vicky gets up in the morning, she begins defrosting or frying. Wednesdays are a problem. It's seniors' day at the movies: a ten o'clock show at two-fifty a ticket, free bagels and coffee; then the senior lunch special at the Taipei Garden, all they can eat for five dollars. Around four-thirty, Vicky is beside herself, left with a gaping hole in her schedule. She wants to make dinner, but they are too stuffed to eat. She can't understand Toni, who often stops by as late as five in the evening on her way home from work and still has no idea of what she's preparing for dinner. Sometimes Vicky thinks that Toni wanted her parents to move to Hazzardville so that Vicky would feed Toni and her children.

"Nobody cooking at your house?" Rocco asks Toni. Or, "Probably getting a pizza," he utters with disgust after she leaves.

The insinuation is that Toni's husband left her because there was no food, when the truth is, it was really Toni who wanted the divorce. It's no wonder she rarely comes around. Rocco manages to alienate everyone; five years in Massachusetts, and they still have no friends. It was Mr. Personality at the Sons of Italy meetings in the beginning. The invitations abounded. But, before long, they all saw that Mr. Personality was really Mr. Blowhard. At least, that's what Vicky surmises, because the invitations eventually stopped. That she never reciprocated didn't help. Face it, she tells herself, they never had real friends as a couple. Before people might have had a chance to uncover the real basis of their marriage, Vicky withdrew. She and Rocco always had their parents, siblings, cousins. They had their daughters. And God knows that was enough.

Her life, however, has finally fallen into a peaceful place. While money had been a struggle throughout their marriage, once they sold the bakery, they found themselves comfortable. They have become set in their ways – used to one another. He has gastrointestinal problems and belches after every few bites. And he farts first thing in the morning. She has hemorrhoids and eats stewed prunes, and she cheats at canasta. They food shop on Mondays. She can follow him on the dance floor. They are a couple: two people individually wrapped in Saran Wrap, and fastened together with a rubber band.

In this university town, surrounded by hamlets of dairy farms, Vicky is uncomfortable, always assuming every other citizen has been highly educated.

So unlike Brooklyn. Even the contractors in this small city are college graduates. Even her plumber, who never gets dirty. Even her hairdresser, who doubles as a psychotherapist. The very name Hazzardville made Vicky reluctant to take up residence here, as though catastrophe lurked behind every corner and would threaten her from the second she touched her toes to the floor in the morning to the moment she safely hid them between the sheets again. But, until now, the only catastrophe had occurred in a hardware store where she purchased a tube of Udder Butter, mistaking the ointment used by farmers to lubricate cow teats for hand cream.

She does like her new home and takes pride in how contemporary she's made it: balloon curtains, white rug, bright floral upholstery, accenting her cherished Chippendale bedroom set and Mediterranean dining room. Still, she keeps it all to herself, hides it from the world like a treasure for no one else to enjoy. She's become like that: savoring gifts Toni gives her in a drawer for so long before she wears them, they often go out of style. Toni is unlike her. Even as a little girl she flung off the old for the new. Slept in a new nightgown that very night. Wore a new dress to school the next morning. Relegated what she had enjoyed up to that day to the bottom of her closet or a bag destined for Goodwill. Maybe that's how she got over her second divorce so easily: as soon as husband-number-two was out the door, she was done with him. *Finito.* Before long, her landscaper boyfriend Omar (who Rocco calls the Lawnmower Man) was on the scene, and it was as though the father of her two children had never existed.

"Victoria? It's Andy. Andy Lingua." The first call had taken her totally by surprise. Her heart rate sped up. She felt her knees giving way.

"Who?"

"It's me, Andrew. But everybody calls me Andy."

The Andrew she had known never allowed her to call him Andy, and insisted on calling her Victoria even against her wishes. Moreover, her Andrew's voice had been robust: this man's was tinny and fragile.

"Everyone calls me Vicky. They always have," she said.

"How are you?" he asked.

"Fine." She tried to mask her nervousness. "And you?"

"I hope it's okay."

"What?"

"That I call."

She glanced into the den. Rocco was absorbed in his program.

"How did you find me?" She spoke softly into the receiver.

"Alma."

"My aunt?"

Vicky hadn't seen her mother's younger sister in years. Alma had been a tramp – ran away with Andrew's married brother Albert; didn't even come to her own sister's funeral.

"She showed up at Albert's wake last week."

"Albert's dead?"

"Isn't almost everyone our age?" He tried to joke. She didn't laugh.

"I asked Alma about you. She knew you'd moved to Massachusetts, although she didn't know where. I looked up the gals you used to work with. Helen was the only one I found still in Brooklyn. Her son lives in the old house now, and she's in a nursing home on Long Island. But, of course, you know all that."

Yes, she knew that. Helen was in the same nursing home her daughter Susan had remained in all these years. The old woman had grown so attached to Susan that when Vicky and Rocco moved to Hazzardville, they decided to leave their daughter there rather than move her to Massachusetts. Vicky visits Susan once a month.

Rocco occasionally goes along, but leaves for a good while and visits the old neighborhood in Brooklyn. He likes to check in on the bakery – see how the new owner is doing, and hope the answer is not well.

"Did you speak to Helen?"

"That's how I got your number. How's your sister Giose and her husband? I can't remember his name."

"It's Larry. Both he and my sister are fine. They live on Long Island too. They're great-grandparents. Their son Rudy has two grandchildren."

"Baby Rudy a grandfather!"

"He gave up the Baby years ago."

"And your parents?"

"Passed away."

"Mine too. Where has all that time gone?" His voice began to quiver and she thought he might burst into tears.

He said that he had married once, to an Irish widow from Boston with six children. That was how he had come to Castleton, a small town south of Boston where he had worked as an accountant. But the new family arrangement had been too much to handle for all of them. The children had abused him, he said, taken advantage of him emotionally and financially. The marriage ended after three years and a hefty settlement.

"Funny, isn't it? Both of us winding up in Massachusetts?" he said.

"Vicky!" Rocco called from the den. "*Jeopardy* is on."

"Coming," she shouted back. "Is this really you, Andrew?" she whispered.

"Yes."

She hung up.

She put her cool hands to her flush face and waited until her heart stopped pounding. She went into the den.

"Who were you talking to?" Rocco asked.

"An old friend."

"What'd she want?"

"He just wanted to chat."

Rocco's eyes grew large with surprise, his mouth tense with annoyance.

"He?"

"I think he's ill. I think he's dying. He's been contacting old friends. You know how it is," she lied.

"And he has to talk to *you*?"

"He's also spoken to Helen."

Vicky made it seem as if it had been more than just to get her number. Besides, she knew the mere mention of her benevolent old friend who looked after Susan would calm him down some.

"Do I know him?"

"Andrew Lingua." She took delight in mumbling nonchalantly, and waited for his reaction.

He knitted his eyebrows, his memory straining to recall

the name. Then his expression saddened as though the devil himself had found him out, and she felt sorry for him. She waited for him to say don't get involved.

"It's nothing. He just needed a friend," she reassured him.

When the phone rang during dinner the following week, she told Andrew that he had the wrong number. But she found herself thinking about him while she prepared meals; at the movie theater on Wednesdays; on the buffet line at the Taipei Garden; while watching *Jeopardy*. He had been so handsome. What would he have looked like now? Maybe he would have become pot-bellied like Rocco. And bald like him too. Maybe his breath would have smelled of rotting yellow teeth, and he would cough up phlegm into a large white linen handkerchief when he laughed like the old friends of her grandfather's she remembered from her childhood. She pictured Raymond Burr as the young powerful Perry Mason and his attractive loyal secretary Della. Then she thought of how she had seen them both in a recent made for-television movie the other night. She shuddered. June Allyson consoled those with leaking bladders in Depend commercials. Jane Powell flashed her false teeth in Polident ads. And they were stars! What would anyone from her past think of her now?

At Christmastime, Vicky received a greeting card addressed to both her and Rocco. Inside the card were five photos of Andrew, taken – according to the notations on the back – within the last three years. Taller than she ever remembered him, this lean body towered next to a blue spruce decorated with red and gold bulbs. She held a magnifying glass over the picture and studied him in detail. His hair was gray but thick and wavy like Andrew's had been. There was a mustache, something Andrew had never worn. She could detect creases in his skin, but no hanging flesh, no jowls. Red-eye and glasses made it impossible to see the color of his eyes. An overpowering sadness dominated his expression despite the smile he wore. She hid the photos and left the card out with the rest of the others they'd received. Rocco never noticed it.

She baked a large box of assorted cookies – butter, macaroons, anisette biscuits, sesame – and sneaked them to the post office when Rocco was at the hospital having his monthly blood pressure check-up. Just this, and it would be the end of it. Just this to ease her conscience, to end the correspondence, for he had begun calling her on a regular basis when Rocco was at the barber's or a Sons of Italy meeting. A good deed; a corporal work of mercy. It was Christmastime. They had so much, yet this man who lived in Castleton seemed to have so little.

"You take the Mass Pike, then 495." Vicky smooths the seat of her dress as she sits beside Toni.

"I have a map."

Toni picks up the large veiny representation of Massachusetts spread out on the floor of the car and puts it onto her lap.

"Let me navigate. You can't read while you're driving."

"Ma, please."

"All right. So you know how to travel. But I'm paying for the tolls."

"Fine. Now tell me what's going on," Toni says, pulling out of the driveway.

"Do you remember Andrew Lingua? Of course, you don't remember him, but you've heard me talk about him to Aunt Giose."

"Your old boyfriend."

"Right."

"You're going to see your old boyfriend?"

"Don't get excited. It's nothing like that. He suffers from depression. Has since World War II. He tried to commit suicide." Vicky's voice quivers. She bites her lip to hold back tears.

"And how do you know this?"

Vicky is quiet for a few seconds.

"He called me yesterday. I didn't know what to do at first. I tried to talk him out of it. I tried not to overreact. I didn't even know if I should take him seriously. After he hung up on me, I phoned the police in Castleton."

"I don't understand. He called you after fifty years to tell you he was committing suicide?"

"We've been in touch. Just by phone. Dad knows. At least he knew about the first time," she says. "It's been going on for awhile – nine months," she murmurs.

"Without Dad's knowing?"

"Yes, I don't think it's bad, do you? Andrew's needed someone to talk to. And I've liked talking to him. Is it bad to have him as a friend?"

"I think it's fine."

"You do?"

Vicky recognizes what Toni is doing. She remembers well doing that herself with Toni when Toni was a teenager: don't pass judgment; just let her talk; keep the lines of communication open.

Vicky tells the whole story from the first day she and Andrew met to yesterday's phone call. Toni nods and encourages her to go on. When Vicky comes to the part about her intimate night with Rocco while she was engaged to Andrew, she embellishes the relationship with more feeling for Rocco than existed.

He had been home on furlough; they had barely known one another. Afterwards, she wrote him overseas, assuring him it had been just that a tryst. But when he returned with all the fingers on his right hand missing, he would not take *no* for an answer.

Vicky makes excuses for Rocco's having revealed the affair to her parents and Andrew. (Vicky's father overturned the kitchen table, slapped her, and called her *puttana*. A shell-shocked Andrew spurned her.) Rocco told out of frustration: he loved me, besides, he had been wounded she tells her daughter. But he did it out of selfishness: he was vindictive, she believes.

"Do you think I've missed something sleeping with just one man all my life?" Vicky asks Toni.

"That's a random question."

Vicky is glad that Toni remains focused on the road. She can't look her in the eye and talk about this.

"Do you?" Vicky needs to know her daughter's opinion.

"If it was good, no. If it was bad, I guess so."

Vicky sighs. She wishes Andrew and she had slept together.

"You know that photo of the sailor kissing the nurse in Times Square on the day of the Japanese surrender," Toni says.

"The *Life Magazine* shot," Vicky recollects.

"I read that they were complete strangers. They just

met for the first time in fifty years because of all the end of this war anniversary hoopla."

"And what happened?"

"They introduced themselves and went back to their own lives."

"He was an Italian fellow, you know," Vicky says. "The sailor, I mean."

The hospital is bleak and dirty: brown vinyl floors, smudged glass doors, marked-up yellow walls. Vicky slips into the first ladies' room she sees to pee. She swats her face with some loose powder from her compact and reapplies her lipstick. With a comb, she fluffs up her bangs.

No one seems to be able to tell them where the intensive care unit is. They wander around the entire second floor before they come upon a sign warning them that no one but relatives are permitted through the locked door. Toni grabs the open door while a visitor exits, and tells the first nurse she sees that Mr. Lingua's sister is here to see him.

Intensive Care is a large room with a nurse's station in the center and small, glass-partitioned sections that line the perimeter. The nurses yell when they speak to the patients, who are hooked up to all sorts of machines and dripping liquids. The patients look ancient: already dead.

Toni tells Vicky that she'll wait for her in the lounge. Vicky is relieved to have the first moment alone with Andrew. Before she leaves, Toni picks a stray thread off of the shoulder of her mother's dress, and Vicky becomes embarrassed because Toni must hear the pounding of her heart.

"You came just in time. Mr. Lingua is about to be moved," a nurse, whose name tag reads Karen Fulgham, says.

"To another room?" Vicky asks.

"To another hospital. Deaconess in Boston. They have a psychiatric unit."

"Can I see him?"

"I think he'd like that very much."

"Andrew, you have a visitor." Ms. Fulgham calls loudly. "He's heavily sedated," she whispers to Vicky who steps into the room the nurse has been guarding.

Andrew is lying on a gurney. A blue and white johnny peeks through the neck opening of a red plaid bathrobe. In his hand, he clutches a small wallet-sized photo of Vicky and Andrew taken before he went overseas. Andrew looks up at Vicky: his eyes are thick and dull from too many drugs, yet his face is without wrinkles, and his square jawline hardly rounded out by the years. He is, indeed, her Andrew. She leans over the gurney and takes his hand. He squeezes it: his grip is remarkably firm.

"I didn't want you to see me like this," he says.

His voice is sluggish. His face is pale and his expression strained. He still seems to be trim although it is difficult to tell since he is lying on his side.

"You mean old?"

"I mean like this."

"Then you shouldn't have called me."

"I never thought Rocco would let you come."

"Rocco had no choice."

She hesitates, then kisses him on his cheek which is damp and salty from countless tears. He does not smell like a hospital, rather soapy, like a newborn.

"Andrew, you didn't do this to get me here, did you?" Vicky says sternly, trying to make him at least smile.

"I never wanted you to see me like this," he repeats.

"As though I look grand," she says flippantly.

"You're more beautiful than I remember you."

"Seeing me hasn't broken the spell?"

"I'm more spellbound than ever."

"You're not wearing your glasses."

"Don't cry, dear," he says.

"My daughter is here. She drove me. Would you like to meet her?"

Vicky asks Ms. Fulgham to bring in Toni; her own legs will not move from the gurney's side. With her free hand she takes a Kleenex from the nightstand.

"She looks just like you," Andrew says when Toni arrives.

"She has her father's coloring." Vicky wipes away tears.

"It's nice to meet you," Toni says, taking his other hand.

"Don't ever grow old, Dear. It's a terrible thing to grow old," he says, staring up into Toni's dark eyes.

"She's ours, isn't she?" Andrew asks Vicky.

"How could she be?" Vicky says, saddened at the thought that he could possess that notion. Wishing that it was the truth.

"It's time," Karen Fulgham announces.

"So soon?" Vicky looks up.

Andrew tightens his grip on Vicky.

"I used to think you were the weak one. But I was wrong. You're strong. You've always been strong," he says.

"And now you need to be strong – for yourself. You need to get well," Vicky tells him.

"Forgive me."

"You've already apologized so many times."

"Only over the phone. I should have married you, Vicky."

"Maybe next time around," she says.

"I'll be waiting for you at the gate."

She wants to kiss him on the lips, but not in front of Toni.

An orderly walks in, and it's all over.

"Let's go, old man," the orderly says, wheeling the gurney towards the door.

Vicky swings around to face the young man. Her lips are taut, her hazel eyes on fire.

"Don't you call him that! He's a hero. He flew thirty missions in World War II. He received the Flying Cross Medal. Don't you dare call him old man."

"I'm sorry, Ma'am," the orderly says, his eyes wide with surprise. "A war hero, huh? I'll take good care of him." He wheels Andrew towards the elevator.

"Are you the one who called the police?" Karen Fulgham asks Vicky.

"Yes."

"You saved his life. He'd taken a lot of pills, but they didn't work. They found a knife in his bed. He meant business. You're the lady in the picture, aren't you? He won't let go of that for anything."

"It's been fifty years," Vicky tells her, as though she herself has just realized it.

"Come on, Ma." Toni takes Vicky's arm.

"In a minute."

Toni goes out in the hall, while Vicky sits down in the black leather armchair that has been expecting her and others like her. The rooms of the IC unit whirl by her like horses on a carousel.

She needs to be still for a moment; it was all too quick for one who seems to have been sitting here, in this chair, waiting, for fifty years. She and Toni had considered stopping for a cup of coffee before they visited Andrew. Vicky can't get over the fact that, but for a few minutes, they would have missed him. Who? Andrew, as she had known him, remembered him, tall and straight and unblemished is gone: in his place exists an old man now on his way to a locked room in Boston. She is numb. And for a few seconds, she cannot imagine any other life of hers, except this hospital, this IC unit, and this chair.

"He's a handsome man," Toni tells her mother in a booth at Friendly's. Vicky wishes Toni wouldn't compliment Andrew. It makes her feel as if her life with Rocco has been even more of a waste than she already believes.

"He was a beautiful man. A beautiful boy with a beautiful soul."

A whole Andrew might have punched Rocco DiBenedetto in the face upon learning what had gone on between him and Vicky. A whole Andrew might have professed his love for Vicky and claimed her despite her fall from grace.

But a broken Andrew, who had spent six months recuperating from battle fatigue in a hospital in Scotland, had merely listened, convinced that the love that had brought him home had been a sham.

"Fucking war. It killed him. It's still killing him. It ruined all of us."

Vicky is more surprised than Toni that she has so easily let "fucking" come rolling out of her mouth this time.

"I don't understand why you married Dad," Toni says.

Vicky takes time to answer this one. Can she explain what it feels like to be trapped by guilt, so trapped that you would give your life to find a way out? That she did, in a way, give her life to make up for what she felt had destroyed her parents' faith in her and Andrew's love. That she had had to do something then and there; that there had been no waiting for time to heal because the luxury of time never existed back then. That it hadn't been so difficult a task because, like Andrew, shock made her unfeeling. There had been no victory in her unconventional behavior with Rocco. There is never victory when others are made to suffer. Can Toni comprehend a world without choice? One always has a choice, Toni will say. And she is right. Vicky had chosen: once to betray and once again to repent by punishing herself and marrying Rocco. Then God sent her Susan. But it still wasn't enough. She inflicted yet more penance upon herself. She denied herself pleasures she once thought she couldn't live without – poetry, theater, the botanical gardens. One by one, with determination, she stripped them and other things from her life like excessive red tape – like Andrew's memory. Soon almost nothing remained except the boring basics. Then Andrew's phone calls began.

"Times were different then," Vicky tells Toni. "My parents were immigrants. They were strict. They had expectations – pride. Everything was about honor and respect. I was young. It was wartime. I made mistakes. But everything wasn't a mistake," she is quick to assure her daughter. "You, your sister."

"Even we didn't make life easy for you."

"Were you uncomfortable today?"

Toni shrugs as if to say some.

"A mother's not supposed to do these things, a mother my age."

"I'm glad you went. You saved his life! That took courage."

"I couldn't let him down – again. Are you and Omar going to get married?"

Vicky feels more at liberty than usual to ask the very private Toni.

"Probably."

"You love him?"

"I think so."

"Differently than your husband?"

"Not like with my first, if we can remember back that far. That was all passion. The second time around was intellectual. I was trying to do the right thing, believe it or not, make you and Dad proud of me. This one is friendship and attraction, but not crazy mad attraction. You know what I mean?"

Vicky knows exactly what she means. That's how she feels about Andrew this very moment.

"The blessing of menopause. You can see men for what they really are," Vicky says.

Toni laughs and Vicky is delighted. She likes Toni, respects her candidness, envies her for having slept with more than one man.

For the first time, it is Vicky who makes the motion to leave. Toni is relaxed and appears to be able to sit like this with her mother forever, and that seems to have made everything in Vicky's life worthwhile.

"My little grandson will be getting home from camp soon," Vicky says.

"He has a key."

"Thank you for taking me, Toni."

"My pleasure, Mom."

The joy of this sudden intimacy between them is almost too much for Vicky who chooses to destroy it rather than experience the pain of Toni or anyone else beating her to it.

"Finish your sandwich." Vicky points to a quarter of a Reuben lying on Toni's plate. "You never finish anything."

"That's not true. Besides, I'm full. I ate the French toast, remember?"

"At least eat the corned beef. It's –"

"Protein."

"I'm paying for lunch," Vicky says.

On the ride home Vicky's thoughts turn to Rocco. She has never really been afraid of him and his rages the way she used to be of her father. Except for one time, when Rocco stabbed an employee at the bakery for stealing and making a fool out of him. The wound was superficial. They settled their differences without the police, since they both would have been arrested: one, for theft; the other, for assault and battery with a deadly weapon. Yet she kept the kitchen knives out of sight for years and held her breath whenever he became frustrated carving the turkey on Thanksgiving Day.

"Don't come in," Vicky tells Toni when they pull up to the house.

Vicky finds Rocco sitting in the den. The television turned off. There is no newspaper on his lap. He comes to life when he sees her.

"It went okay?" he asks.

"Yes."

"He's all right?"

"He's in a psychiatric hospital."

"Did you get lost?"

"No."

TICKET TO RIDE

Where am I now? I need to know. Between the darkness and Cousin Brucie's irritating voice on the radio, and my mother sitting beside me – her overnight bag on the backseat – I've grown unconscious of my whereabouts traveling north on Interstate 95. Exit 16. Norwalk. I'm in Norwalk, Connecticut, the sign tells me. In two hours and ten minutes I'll arrive home with my mother who, after fifty-two years, has left my father.

We were at my younger brother Robert's apartment in SoHo tonight to celebrate his thirty-fifth birthday. My brothers are lucky. While they never liked having two first names anymore than I did, at least each of theirs were different. I, however, had been our parents' second child, and until Robert came along, their creative genius seemed to have exhausted itself with the naming of my older brother Ernest. They called me Gordon. Gordon Gordon.

"Would you have preferred that we call you Flash?" my mother always responded to my childhood complaints, as though Flash would have been the only alternative. "You weren't the most alert infant in the nursery, and we thought that learning one name would make it easier on you."

I must have been nothing short of dead, a one out of ten on the Apgar score, to warrant that action. Perhaps my mother had been right, because I could write my name at age three, my full name, forward *and* backward. My mother attributed my intelligence to the fact that my name had been so simple: it hadn't cluttered my mind. My mother also believes that white bread is healthier when toasted because it is brown and that the Internet is a new form of transportation intended to replace the Brooklyn Bridge.

Robert's apartment takes up the entire third floor of a converted office building. It's so like Robert to have more than he needs: three baths, four bedrooms, a living room that could contain the entire first floor of my modest New England saltbox. But then again, Robert has always taken up a lot of space in my family. If it weren't for Robert, sometimes I wonder whether or not my mother would ever have gotten up in the morning all these years. She is obsessed with him. Always has been. Since his untimely birth in the twilight of her fertile years had not been planned, my mother assumed her conception to be a directive from God to right all of my father's and her past wrongdoings around parenthood. I had been smart, but my intelligence must have been limited, according to my mother, and certainly not cultivated since I never aspired to anything more than a social worker, a pseudoshrink as my father calls it. Poor Ernest. His brains were considered to be nonexistent the first time he tried to swing from our sixth story apartment window to the one across the alley on a knotted series of my mother's best sheets, and wearing nothing more than a loin cloth fashioned from Fruit of the Loom's basic white brief line.

On the other hand, Robert the Gift was gifted, or so he'd been told from birth. And to the gifted must come privilege. And because of privilege, comes neglect to others – namely Ernest and me. Don't get me wrong. I love my brother Robert. He's charming and good looking to boot. And he's really quite kind, would give you the Armani suit right off his back as soon as it got a stain on it. His high opinion of himself is not really obnoxious either, maybe even healthy. Robert is the poster boy of positive thinking, the proof that most of what you are is what you've been told that you are.

This entire evening my father complained about how the music, a mix tape Robert's girlfriend had made, was too loud. "Can't you remember being young?" my mother asked my father. He didn't answer, as though he has no memory of anything at all. Rather, he looked at her even more disgustedly than she had looked at him and continued to sit in the corner of the wall farthest from the boom box, reading the lips of anyone who engaged him in conversation. He sat isolated from my mother, who tried ever so feebly to mingle with Robert's sophisticated Wall Street colleagues. She invited them to eat as though she had hosted the party herself. "Have some cake," she urged, gesturing to the table covered with a purple crepe paper tablecloth and pushed up against the wall. The rectangular sheet cake was enormous, way too large for the number of people at the party. It sat in the center and covered most of the table's surface. Robert's girlfriend ordered it. She ordered everything from an upscale caterer on Spring Street. Aside from the large colorful Italian plates it was attractively arranged on, it amounted to nothing more than chips and salsa, hummus and pita bread, prosciuto rolled around melon chunks, and a plate of endive leaves with a dollop of curry dip spattered on the edge of each leaf. My wife Lorraine, who is home sick with the flu, could have whipped this all up in half and hour. The icing on the cake was purple. So were the streamers Robert's girlfriend had hung crisscrossed from the corners of the ceiling. Robert's girlfriend is a blond he met at the Ralph Polo Lauren men's cosmetic counter at Bloomingdales where she works. Robert says she's really a writer. If she has anything to say, she's keeping it all inside, because although her smile is engaging and her turquoise eyes captivating, with the exception of desperately inquiring where Robert is when out of her sight, I have only heard her speak in monosyllables. She's Scandanavian, Robert has offered in her defense. This is true, but she was born in Queens.

I glanced into the corner of the room where my father sat with his empty stomach spilling over his alligator belt, his jowls straining for his shoulders, his once well-defined nose growing larger by the second, porous and without definition, and I believed that *he* – or fear of becoming like him – was the root of all my problems. Apparently my father got to my mother too this evening. When my brother Robert stood in the center of the room and humbly (which only made him more attractive) thanked everyone for coming, my mother stepped up beside him and announced to an attentive crowd of virtual strangers that she was divorcing my father and coming home with me tonight to Massachusetts.

"You're joking, Mom," Robert, the Cornell graduate, tried to dismiss her as though she had pulled his pants down in front of his friends.

"There's no Tupperware in that overnight bag you brought, is there, Ma?" Ernest the cop interrogated my mother.

"No." She took her black and white nylon duffle bag – *Foxwoods* written across it – from Robert's broom cabinet.

"You knew!" Robert accused Ernest.

"She said it was Tupperware for the leftovers."

"You should have known," I said. "You're a cop."

"Was I supposed to frisk her?"

"I'll wait for you downstairs, Gordon." My mother walked out.

Nobody tried to stop her. We just went on about who should have known first and how embarrassing this all was for Robert.

By the time my mother and I arrive at my house tonight, Lorraine will be in bed although she isn't really sick. I haven't told my family yet, but we too have decided to separate.

Lorraine and I met in college in the second semester of our junior year at Stonybrook. She was an aspiring physical therapist who'd known what she wanted to do ever since she'd seen *Amahl and the Night Visitors* on television when she was five. She renamed all of her dolls Amahl and spent the next thirteen years manipulating their limbs in an effort to cure the various debilitating ailments her imagination inflicted upon them. Due to my talent for mimicry, languages came easily to me. I became a Spanish major, who had not the faintest notion of what he would do with this foreign tongue, besides teach it to more floundering souls who wouldn't know what to do with it. While I enjoyed Cervantes and Lope de Vega, I couldn't imagine there was much more to uncover about their writing that hadn't already been divulged over the past five hundred years. Such was my limited perception of the world. But Lorraine, like the jaws of life, pried away at me with her constant suggestions until I believed that working with inner-city youths who are at risk would satisfy all: my language skills; her compassion for the underdog.

When a teaching assistantship for a Master's degree in social work was offered to me at Boston College, my (or rather Lorraine's) plans for reconstructing the ills of ghetto upbringing remained on Long Island, while I proceeded to hide behind the gates of academia until I reached the end of the matriculating line – a Ph.D. I have, nevertheless, managed to remain behind the ivy covered walls of a small college in Western Massachusetts where I teach disciples, who possess much more chutzpa than I do, to take out into the world what I tell them. Lorraine works in the physical therapy department of a hospital, not the local one in town, but one in a nearby city with a large Puerto Rican population. She has learned Spanish through in-service courses, tapes, and continuing education classes. Lorraine and I lived together after college for three years; we were in no hurry to become stayed. We married when we were twenty-five.

Cousin Brucie plays a Beatles' tune, "Ticket to Ride." Brucie used to play more 1950s and very early 1960s music: more Motown, Bobby Rydell, The Shirells. "FM 101.1 The station with a million memories," he claims in an intense raspy voice that hasn't changed in over thirty-five years. The Beatles are hardly oldies to me but, at forty-nine, I can't manage to regard myself as middle aged either. I am in the old age of youth. And Cousin Brucie? That guy must be almost my mother's vintage by now. But that's the beauty of radio – makes us all deniers.

"The Beatles were great," my mother says. "Nowadays all they sing is noise."

Funny. That's what she used to say about the Beatles when they first came on the scene. Nonsensical lyrics. Have you ever listened to the words to a Perry Como song? "What did Delaware? She wore a brand New Jersey or Hot diggity dog diggity boom what you do to me, boom it's so new to me, boom what you do to me." Yet his show was the highlight of my parents' Saturday night for years. I have to admit that I like Sinatra, own some of his CDs. Big band CDs too. So my mother now likes some of the music of my time, and I like some of the music of her time, but we both hate most of today's music that I will probably love in thirty years. Which only goes to prove the point: how can you trust your judgments? When will a decision in the present become the nightmare of the future? And how can you know?

"You're all better looking than they were," my mother says.

"Than who?"

"The Beatles. Your brothers and you are much better looking."

"So what?"

"They were so popular. But you were much better looking."

"They could sing, Mom. We can't even hum."

She shrugs her shoulders. She has acquired the habit of drawing parallels between everything and her sons: "The President's State of the Union message was good, but

Robert spoke better at your grandmother's funeral;" Al Pacino is a good actor, but you have a nicer nose."

"Why do you have to compare everyone else to us? One has nothing to do with the other," I say.

She thinks for a moment. "How would I relate to anything if it wasn't through my children, my family? I never went to college. Can I say that I disagree with a Supreme Court ruling?"

"Hell, yes."

"No, Gordon. I'm not qualified. Am I a judge? I'm not even a lawyer. But your brother Robert – even you – have education. The admittance of my intelligence and Robert's in almost the same breath nearly made me pull over and hug her.

"What about Ernest?" I already know her response.

"Ernest can say what he pleases. He's a cop."

My grandmother did a job on my mother. The old German woman was built like a giant *spatzle*, but that's as far as her softness went. A veritable despot, she was determined to undermine her only daughter's every move. The soup was always too salty, the rice too sticky, the couch she purchased too cheap, the rug too expensive. My mother was afraid to make a move. When I was little, I liked the way my grandmother cut my mother down: justice for some disciplining my mother had performed. But as I grew older, the bullets the old lady shot at my mother made me cringe with discomfort; my mother's lack of self-confidence pained and at the same time annoyed me. She couldn't even hang a picture without advice: here or two inches below? And I became afraid. What if I did that to one of my offspring? So much power in parenting. One's relationship with his or her spouse had to be strong to rear children: there was no room for dissension; the slightest weakening of the conjugal bond could rupture into a massive pool of blood within which a confused and misguided child might drown, be lost forever. The responsibility wrapped itself around me like a rag soaked in ether, and the mention of children nearly caused me to hit the deck, lose my cookies. Lorraine and I were not perfect. I knew it; she knew it. Only she accepted it, whereas I could not. The potential for divorce was always there, like a canvas backdrop waiting to be released behind our domestic scene, drastically altering its direction for good. "This is true of all relationships," Lorraine would say. Such a notion only confirmed my terror. After all, what had my mother learned from her experience with *her* mother? Up until a minute ago – nothing.

"I don't like the way you drive," my mother tells me, as though feeling a need to take back her compliment about my intelligence. And I retrieve mine. What has my mother learned from her experience with her mother? Nothing.

The music is becoming filled with static. I need to change the station, find a local one, but I can't let go of Cousin Brucie.

My brother Ernest and I used to share a transistor radio when we were growing up in Brooklyn. On summer days, we carried it to the elementary school where we shot baskets inside the small but cool gymnasium. We brought it on the train that took us from Boro Park to Coney Island. We protected it from sand on a beach blanket on Bay 15, while trying to kiss Maxine Reiss and Marie Grillo without cutting our lips on their braces. We kept it on the floor between our twin beds at night until we fell asleep to the grating, yet seductive voice of a DJ named Bruce Morrow who would tell us, no shout at us, over and over again that he was our Cousin Brucie. A million memories all right. That's when the biggest decisions facing us were whether to root for the Yankees or St. Louis, or to make the one fast dance we dared at the party a cha cha or the twist. Decisions that felt ladened with consequences. Consequences that had the life-span of about five minutes. I never wanted Brucie to be my cousin. I wanted him to be my father.

"What's that?" my mother becomes startled.

"The cell phone."

"Why do you need one of those things in the car? You're not a doctor."

"Actually I am."

"I mean a real doctor. Besides, those phones are dangerous. And expensive."

"You have no idea what they cost."

"They must be expensive."

"It's Ernest."

"He has your number here?"

Ernest wants to know what the hell is going on. How could I have agreed to take my mother back home with me. I tell him that I didn't agree; she just got into the car. What was I supposed to do? Leave my seventy-nine-year-old mother in tears, sitting on her Foxwoods bag at the corner of Thompson Street and Sixth Avenue, while taxis dropped off groups of chic twenty-somethings to gape at her on their way into the Veruka Club?

"Turn around and come back. Dad's a wreck," Ernest says.

"I don't believe it. He didn't say a word when she left."

"He was in shock. Actually he's snoring here on Robert's couch."

"Cutting into Robert's plans for the evening?"

"Listen, Gordon. Jeannie and I need to get home tonight."

"What's the rush? You got babies waiting for you? Your daughter's at Tulane and your son's on a safari in Kenya."

"Where are you, Gordon, in New Rochelle? If you don't turn the fucking car around, I'm gonna call a buddy of mine who's a desk officer on the Westchester P.D. and *he'll* have you stopped and turned around."

"Too late. I'm already in Connecticut."

"You're speeding."

"You're right. Here's Mom."

"What do I do with it?" she says, taking the phone.

"Just hold it like a regular phone and talk."

"No, Ernest. I'm not coming back, I don't care what any of you boys say. Not even Robert."

"Good, because he's probably too busy to get on the phone," I tell her.

I can swear that Lorraine had accepted my refusal to have children, even agreed with it a long time ago. In the beginning of our marriage she would bring it up, but then there was no more mention of it: she had her work; we had our friends, nieces and nephews. I must have wanted to ignore the sadness in her eyes whenever cherub figures in rosebud flannel nightgowns or Superman pajamas floated in and out of our friends' living rooms looking for attention. I must have wanted to miss the tenseness in her smile when we all clapped at their awkwardly choreographed dance routines, simple melodies sung out of tune, stand-up knock-knock jokes. I must have not seen her looking the other way when these little fairies were scooped up by Mommy or Daddy and, sleepy heads nuzzling into strong shoulders, were carried up to bed. Perhaps she had not screamed out her pain because the possibility had still been there – to have children, that is, to persuade me. She must have borne that hope like a pregnant woman bears a fetus, only her gestation period had gone on for twenty-four years. Then, oddly, when it seemed as though we were on par with everyone else, when other homes were becoming as quiet as ours, with children off at college or making their way in more exciting territory, when women no longer spoke about babysitters and PTA fundraisers but night sweats and hormone replacement, when their concerns had finally become hers, she became depressed, then angry. "You could have had one," she told me at Ernest's son's graduation. "You could have had one," she whispered as her brother walked his daughter down the aisle.

It appeared that when the potential for having a child no longer existed, along with it had gone Lorraine's acceptance – or tolerance – of being childless. Before long she grew more and more distant, unable to conceal her distaste when I walked into a room or came to bed. Twenty-four years plus, and her eyes asked: Who are you? What have I done? Just when I was about to suggest that we see a marriage counselor, she seemed to be having second thoughts (maybe I should call them third thoughts), coming around, being her rational self. That's when her friend Dorothy Robinson, a high school principal into the extrasensory, introduced her to a medium in Upstate New

York. It was a lark at first, a harmless spring fling. Lorraine had always laughed at Dionne Warwick's charlatan psychics – worse than Gypsy fortune tellers, she had said. Lorraine was a woman of science. But before long, she was on the phone with this woman, whispering behind closed doors at all hours of the night. She made special trips to see her. "She's helping me," she said. With what? I wanted to know. "Our differences. Our future. She sees the truth," she replied. A week ago, she announced that she could no longer live with a man who had robbed her; she had made enough of a mistake wasting so many years. If I had denied her a child, I never could have really loved her, and that was the bottom line – I had betrayed her. Somehow Lorraine had let the psychic give her license to deal with her resentment by disposing of me and negating anything good that had ever happened between us. It was too late for therapy: when Lorraine's biological clock stopped ticking, our marriage stopped tocking.

I visited this medium last week, intending to smash her crystal ball into smithereens, to tear up her tarot cards, tell her to go to hell. There was no crystal ball nor any tarot cards. She was a handsome woman around sixty with long silvery hair and steel-gray eyes that cut me down quicker than a laser beam. She sat on a wicker chair on her porch that summer evening, wearing a long Indian print dress and, to the shrill sound of cicadas, told me in few words that I was no friend of my wife's. The woman was disarming, and I, Dr. Gordon, had been prepared to battle. She had caught Lorraine off guard, however, found her vulnerability and pecked at it, perforating our marriage until it could no longer stand on its own and all that remained of our relationship was a gaping hole:

twenty-four years of togetherness reduced to little more than a juicy story to be ooed and ahed over and analyzed in front of the granola bins at the health food store. What satisfaction had this woman gotten out of taking my wife from me? What had she seen about me, uncovered to Lorraine, that I had been able to get away with for more than twenty-four years?

I shift in my seat and unfasten my seat belt, as though what I have to say to my mother cannot come out under such constraints.

"Why, Mom? Why are you doing this?"

"Oh, Gordon, you know how he's always put me down. The way he used to knock my cooking, then praise that floozie who lived next door to us like she was Julia Child. You know the one."

"Gladys Stein."

"She had that brassy bleached red hair."

"Gladys Stein."

"All she ever made was that lousy pot roast that stank up the hallway until you wanted to puke. She was a Jewish woman."

"Gladys Stein."

"Oh well, her name will come to me."

"But, Mom, admit it. You had a habit of serving him dishes he hated. Sometimes, I thought you even delighted in it."

"That's not true, Gordon. I just wanted him to acquire a taste for more than pot roast. And I tried to keep a clean house, but he never appreciated it. The last fifteen years have been hell with his collections. It's as though he went off the deep end, afraid to get rid of anything: a piece of junk mail, a newspaper. He has a hard time returning library books. He calls himself a collector. He's a slob."

"Anal retentive."

"You know what it is, Gordon? I finally figured it out. He fears death."

I have to acknowledge that she might be on to something.

"And now he says I'm dirty. Of course, I quit cleaning. How can you clean when you have to walk through paths of *Handyman* four-feet high? I'll tell you something that I'm ashamed of. We have to go to the YMCA to shower."

"Whatever for?"

"He refuses to remove the piles of junk he has in the bathtub. Ancient business ledgers, his old plumber's tools, you name it."

The house has been trashed of late, so much so that my brothers and I offered to haul everything down to the dumpster. My father, in his fashion, never really said much; it was my mother who voiced the loudest objection. I figured that my mother and he were both just growing crazy together. Now, I realize that she had always felt a need to cover for him for some reason – to cover for all of us. The bathtub was news, however, since the pink plastic shower curtain with black swans was always drawn tightly across the tub when we used the john.

"When he started accusing me of trying to poison him, that was the last straw."

"How long has that been going on?" I am rather incredulous.

"Awhile, Gordon. A good while. Arsenic in his Cream of Wheat, cyanide in his Metamucil."

"But you must be able to work this out some way. After all these years. Shit, you're in your eighties."

"Your father is eighty-three. I'm still finishing my seventy-ninth year. But what does that matter? You think you lose your feelings at this age? Eyesight, yes; energy, yes; feelings, never. And memory. People think because you can't remember what happened yesterday, you've forgotten the last fifty-two years together. But you never forget some things, Gordon. Never."

My stomach muscles tighten to the point that I feel they might break through my skin like aliens, bringing out with them all my ugliness – all of Lorraine's memory. When did my mother become Sigmund Freud?

"I should have done this a long time ago. Maybe I've finally become a modern woman. I won't take anymore."

The phone she's been holding in her hand like a new toy rings; she jumps.

"Would you answer it please, Mom."

"What do I do?"

"Just press *Send*."

"Hello, this is the Gordon Car," she says in her secretarial voice.

"Beverly? It's Herb." I can hear my father shouting louder than usual into his receiver since he's talking to a moving vehicle.

"I know who you are," she says.

I tune out their conversation and try to concentrate on the music, but the static has taken over. I scan the stations until a French one from Quebec somehow manages to come in. I'd rather not understand what anyone is saying right now. I picture Lorraine, her smooth sandy hair falling over her freckled face as she sleeps. Or maybe she's reading or getting ready for *Mad TV*. She's happy that I'm gone, can't wait until I've moved out for good. I should feel victory: my greatest fear of my marriage ending has finally come to fruition. But I'm not enjoying victory anymore than I can accept that my marriage is over. I guess I have my mother to thank for believing that relationships should be maintenance-free, and for making me oblivious to a wife who had been doing all of the repair work on mine. Who am I kidding? It was up to me to recognize that my love, not hers, was conditional. Up to me to accept, as she did, our imperfection. To sacrifice as she did. To feel as good as my brother Robert. To change my first name. I never missed having children, yet if Lorraine and I *had* had them, just one, there would be something there to connect us, even in divorce: a son who prefers Cousin Brucie to his father is still a son. But I have never been good at creating. Whether deserving or not, I stand helpless now. And that is the most painful. The worst.

"How do I hang up, Gordon?"

"Press the *End* button."

"Your father apologized," she says in amazement. "He wants me to come home. This is the first time he's apologized in fifty-two years."

"Shall I turn around?"

"Would you mind? Ernest and Jeannie are waiting to drive us home. I know it's awfully late for you. Lorraine will worry. You can call her!" She offers me the phone, pleased with her idea.

"She's probably already asleep. I told you she wasn't feeling well." I still can't bring myself to tell my mother about us. Not right now. I'll probably crash on Robert's Italian leather couch. Or maybe I'll turn right around again and drive home, no matter what hour of the morning it is. Maybe I'll just keep driving until I reach the Cape and sleep on White Crest Beach, protected by the ocean on one side and the massive dunes on the other. Maybe I'll be lifted up out of sight with the early morning fog, leaving behind no heirs possessing my chin line, not a trace.

I get off at the next exit and make my way back onto the southbound lane. My mother is happy, humming along to some French melody she seems to recognize. A war tune she says. I'd like to call Lorraine, to hear her voice, to relate the evening's events. I'd like to apologize. Not that I haven't already done that, though my apologies always demanded that she accept some of the blame. But I know that an apology would be of no use tonight, even an unconditional one. We've gone over the edge. My ticket to ride has expired. I lost Cousin Brucie somewhere around Exit 40.

Printed in January 2007 at Gauvin Press, Gatineau, Québec